Queen in Waiting

Queen in Waiting

A Life of "Bloody Mary" Tudor

A Project of WomenWhoLead.org

by Georgess McHargue

iUniverse, Inc.
New York   Lincoln   Shanghai

Queen in Waiting
A Life of "Bloody Mary" Tudor

iUniverse, Inc.

For information address:
iUniverse, Inc.
2021 Pine Lake Road, Suite 100
Lincoln, NE 68512
www.iuniverse.com

0-595-31254-3

Dedication

This book is dedicated to my daughter Mairi so she can finally finish her seventh-grade summer reading, and to the board members of WomenWhoLead.org, Carol Antos, Cindy Beams, Marty Green, and Aleta Manugian. They shared my determination that the life stories of women leaders should not be erased from history.

Contents

Acknowledgments

WomenWhoLead.org wishes to express its gratitude to the many people who helped bring this book to completion. Our thanks to Nan Harbison for preparing the graphics for publication; to Jane Orner for designing the cover; to Michael Roberts and Paul Green for technical assistance; to Sanderson Associates for the maps and genealogical charts; to Sharon Wooding for the cover illustration; and to many donors for supporting the development of this and future volumes.

Mary Tudor at the age of twenty-eight.
(By courtesy of the National Portrait Gallery, London)

Chapter 1

"Right High, Right Noble, and Right Excellent"

A silver font held the water for her christening. The church was bright with cloths and draperies embroidered with jewels and pearls. A countess carried her to the church. A cardinal—a prince of the Roman Catholic Church—was her godfather. Her three godmothers were a king's daughter, a king's niece, and a duchess. She was named Mary after her father's favorite sister. Immediately, the royal heralds came forward to proclaim her "the right high, right noble, and right excellent princess of England and daughter of our sovereign lord the king." It was February 20, 1516, and the place was Greenwich, England.

Probably, none of the nobles, priests, or servants at the christening foresaw that this tiny child, just three days old, would someday rule England. In all of English history, only one woman had ever claimed the throne, and that had been nearly four hundred years earlier. Besides, that luckless queen had lost the crown to her male cousin after a bloody civil war. So, although there was no law forbidding a woman to rule England, as there was in nearby France, the crowd of powerful nobles in the church never imagined that they were attending the christening of their future sovereign.

For one thing, little Mary's parents, King Henry VIII and Queen Katharine, fully intended to have more children. Surely, they told themselves, the next child would be a son to follow Henry on the throne.

Katharine had already borne two baby boys, but they had died, a great sorrow to all. Still, their births proved that Katharine could have sons. So Mary's future was clear in everyone's mind. She would marry a foreign king or prince and bring honor and security to England by doing so. But her own decisions and desires would leave no mark on history. Power was for princes, not princesses.

For now, the baby Mary would live the life of an English princess. From the beginning, she would have her own household of servants, waiting women, and officials. Three of these are listed in the records of the time as "rockers," a title that suggests their main duty was simply to rock Mary's splendid cradle. Her royal parents—or their servants—had foreseen every possible need of this very special baby.

Detail of a painted parchment roll showing King Henry riding in a tournament while Queen Katharine and other spectators watch. Henry's horse cloths are marked with Katharine's initial, K.

(Westminster Tournament Roll, by courtesy of the College of Arms, London)

Mary's parents were two rather remarkable people, and not merely because they were king and queen. Mary's mother, Katharine, had been a Spanish princess. She is usually known as Katharine of Aragon, which was a part of Spain. Katharine was the youngest daughter of the renowned Queen Isabella of Castile, who had funded the voyages of Christopher Columbus. Isabella had not been a stay-at-home queen. She had ridden at the head of her own armies. In fact, Katharine had been born in a military camp while her mother was directing the siege of a major city. (There is a chart showing Mary's family tree at the end of this book.)

Isabella also respected learning, and she made sure her daughters had far better educations than the average princesses of their time. She brought famous thinkers to her court, including the notable woman scholar Beatrix Galindo, who was a professor of Latin and Philosophy at the Spanish University of Salamanca. Beatrix taught Latin to Isabella's children, both princes and princesses. Not that the girls were brought up to rule—they were destined for the royal marriage market, like all princesses. Still, Isabella's daughters learned a great deal more than the usual needlework, music, and court manners of noble young ladies.

When her father and mother arranged an English marriage for her, Katharine made no protest. Petite, blonde, and round-faced, Katharine had all the love of ceremony and good manners for which the Spanish court was famous. The English people thought her queenly, sweet, and in every way a proper wife for their young king. That Katharine also possessed great strength of character was revealed only later.

While Princess Mary's mother was well educated, her father Henry was considered brilliant. In his youth, all Europe had applauded this tall, red-haired prince's accomplishments. He could argue philosophy with scholars in several languages, ride off to the hunt, play tennis, win the prize at a tournament, and dance all evening. He loved music and composed several instrumental pieces and love songs that are still performed today. Besides excelling at sports, music, and learning, Henry had a fun-loving streak that his subjects found endearing. In his youth they had nicknamed him Prince Hal. Henry liked nothing better than to dress himself and his men in outlandish costumes and appear suddenly in the midst of some court occasion. Once, disguised as Robin Hood and his Merry Men, they even invaded the queen's private rooms. But Katharine, who knew her husband's ways, was quick to see through the trick and play along, to the great amusement of all.

Yet underneath the brilliance, a hidden insecurity dogged Henry's reign. He was only the second member of the Tudor family to wear the crown. His own father, King Henry VII, had not inherited the throne, but won it on the battlefield. As kings, the Tudors were upstarts; and they were surrounded by nobles who traced their families back for centuries. To strengthen his position, Henry VIII needed a healthy son—better yet, two or three sons.

These two people, the 25-year-old king and the 31-year-old queen, may have been royalty, but they were also parents. All the evidence suggests that they loved their little daughter Mary very much. Proud father Henry liked to show the baby to visitors, boasting, "This little girl never cries." Mary's parents did everything to ensure her welfare. But "everything" did not mean spending much time with their child. From the first, Mary was cared for by her nursemaids and her "Lady Governess," Margaret Pole, Countess of Salisbury. She did not often see her royal parents in person.

For one thing, the royal life was one of constant travel. The court seldom spent more than a month or so in one place. No single town or village could long provide for so many courtiers and servants. Furthermore, in those days without plumbing, when floors of even the greatest houses were still covered with rushes to absorb food scraps and other trash, any given palace quickly became just too smelly. The only thing to do was to pack up and move on, so that servants could sweep the place clean and air it out. Then, too, the world was full of diseases, and Mary's father Henry worried a lot about the dangers of smallpox, fevers, and the plague, to mention just a few of the illnesses that could kill a person suddenly. Among the most feared was the sweating sickness, a new and terrifying disease. Many of its victims died, "some within three hours, some within two hours, some merry at dinner and dead at supper." When illnesses like these appeared, noble households quickly moved elsewhere. (Ordinary people, of course, had to stay at home and take their chances.)

King Henry VII, Mary's grandfather. Note his resemblance to Prince Arthur, page 17. Arthur's brother, Henry VIII, was cut to a different pattern.
(A.F. Pollard, *Henry VIII*, 1902)

For all these reasons, it was the custom for a royal child to be moved here and there, up and down the kingdom, wherever the climate seemed healthful or the countryside pleasant. There is no complete record of all the places where Mary stayed during her childhood, but she probably never spent more than a few months each year in the company of her parents. Nevertheless, she was raised to be a royal princess from the first—which means she was treated as a tiny adult. For example, there is a surviving list of New Year's gifts from 1523, when Mary was six. (People gave gifts on New Year's Day then, not at Christmas.) The list shows no dolls, toys, or games for Mary. Instead, her father gave her a tall silver cup overflowing with coins. His powerful and ambitious chief official, Lord Chancellor Cardinal Wolsey, gave her a gold salt dish set with pearls. The Countess of Devon offered a gold cross. And a more practical-minded nobleman gave her twelve pairs of shoes. The most touching gift, and perhaps the most interesting one to a child, came from "a poor woman of Greenwich," who brought the princess a potted rosemary bush decorated with silver spangles.

Thus from a very early age Mary was expected to act and perhaps think like a much older person. She learned to walk and talk like any toddler, but she had other tasks as well. Apparently, she inherited her father's love of music and learned that part of her lessons quickly. She also began, at an early age, to learn Spanish (from her mother and her Spanish ladies) and Latin, which was the formal language of the Church and of international affairs.

In addition, Mary began to play her role in the royal marriage game. When she was only two, she was betrothed (that is, engaged) to the small son of the King of France, who was even younger than she. Dressed in cloth-of-gold, with a little black cap of jeweled velvet, Mary behaved well throughout the long ceremony, which included a sermon on the virtues of marriage and ended when Cardinal Wolsey placed a large diamond ring on her tiny finger.

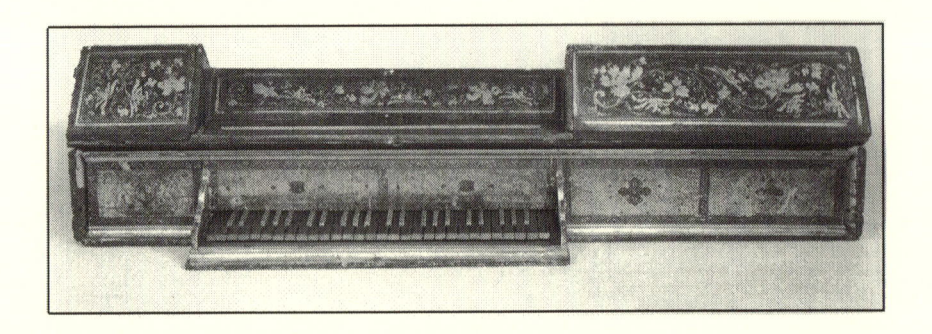

The virginals that Mary played were similar to this set, which belonged to her younger sister, Elizabeth.
(By courtesy of the Victoria and Albert Museum)

After this event, the French took a keen interest in Mary's welfare and development. In 1520, three French courtiers came to see her and were impressed by how well she played the virginals, a small, portable keyboard instrument somewhat like the electronic ones in use today. The gentlemen wrote of her "proper communication and pleasant pastime," so it appears that the little four-year-old girl was not too shy to talk to them. But Mary's betrothal to the little French prince did not last.

The kingdom of France had a powerful rival called the Holy Roman Empire, a now-vanished state that included parts of Germany, northern France, Holland, and Belgium. The ruler of the Holy Roman Empire was Charles V of the Habsburg family, who had recently inherited the crown of Spain as well. King Henry's goal was to gain advantage for England by playing France and the Habsburg Dominions against each other. For most of the 1500s, these three mighty powers carried on a diplomatic game in which any two were perpetually threatening to join against the third. But none of these alliances lasted very long, and the players frequently changed partners. The prizes in this three-sided game were marriages, treaties, trade, and territory, which each player first offered and then withdrew.

By 1520, Henry was already secretly planning to break the French engagement and betroth Mary to Charles V, the Holy Roman Emperor. Charles was twenty, and Mary was only four; but such an age difference was no barrier to royal marriages. Neither was the fact that Charles was Mary's first cousin. His mother was Katharine of Aragon's older sister. But when important people were involved, the pope—as head of the Roman Catholic Church—often gave special permission (called a dispensation) for marriages between relatives.

Henry signed a betrothal agreement with Charles in 1521, and the emperor later visited England to meet his little fiancée. This meeting was brief, but it apparently meant something special to Mary, by then six years old. We don't know what happened when they met, but Mary had a life-long fondness for Charles. The fact that Charles later broke the betrothal agreement doesn't seem to have changed Mary's favorable view of him.

At the same time, however, there was a third plan for Mary's future. Her father was toying with the idea of marrying her to the King of Scots. Scotland was England's neighbor to the north, and a traditional enemy. This marriage, Henry thought, would be a good way to stop the constant threat of Scottish attacks along his northern border.

And so the game went on. Possibly, Mary herself knew little of the turn-abouts in her father's marriage plans for her. She learned early that betrothals came and went. If you didn't like the proposed groom, you had only to wait a few months for somebody else to come along. Meanwhile she lived happily at one or another of her many country houses, learning to ride, make music, sew, read, dance, and know the proper titles of kings, dukes, and lords.

The highlights of Mary's year were her regular holiday visits to the court at Christmas and Easter. The twelve-day Christmas celebration, especially, presented an exciting whirl of color and sound after her peaceful life in the country. During this special season, the court cast off some of its formal manners. The fun was organized by a "Lord of Misrule," a prankster who was allowed to turn things more or less upside-down. He could poke fun at the wealthy, honor servants above their masters, mock important officials, and get away with behavior that would lead to jail or a whipping at other seasons. The whole court followed his lead. Throughout the twelve days, the court was entertained by dancers, jugglers, performing animals, and pageants in which the high and the mighty appeared in colorful costumes and fanciful masks. Mary herself would take part in such "maskings," as they were called, when she was a little older.

Whatever the season, the most important event of Mary's early years was really something that did *not* happen. Although Queen Katharine had at least one pregnancy after 1516, she bore no more living children. There was no little prince to inherit Henry's kingdom.

Of course, it was not strictly true to say that Henry had no sons. In 1519, a woman named Bessie Blount had borne the king a baby boy who was called Henry Fitzroy. (The name Fitzroy came from the French *fils du roi,* which means "son of the king.") Queens in those days were supposed to overlook their husbands' love affairs, and Katharine was no exception. The presence of a royal mistress or two was generally expected at court. Though her feelings might be hurt, Katharine knew that she, and she alone, was the queen. Such romances did not threaten the queen's status. Nor did little Henry Fitzroy, born out of wedlock, threaten Mary's position as heir to the throne.

A miniature of Henry Fitzroy, Duke of Richmond. Although he was the king's son, he could not inherit the throne, as he was born out of wedlock.

(A. F. Pollard, *Henry VIII*, 1902)

With her husband's attention wandering to younger women, Queen Katharine naturally focused more and more of her love on her only child. Mary might be halfway across England, but her mother wrote her many letters, in Spanish, Latin or English. One of Katharine's letters, written when Mary was nine, asked to see the written lessons that Mary was doing for her schoolmaster, John Fetherstone. Like her own mother Isabella, Katharine believed that learning was important for a princess.

It is difficult to know who Mary's friends were during this early period. Did she share her lessons with other children, sons and daughters of her household officers and waiting women? Or was she largely alone? The records make no mention of any playmates of her own age. She did, however, become deeply fond of her governess, Margaret Pole, Countess of Salisbury. The countess herself was of royal descent—two of her uncles had been kings before the Tudors came to power (although it could be dangerous, in Tudor times, to have the blood of older royalty in your veins.) Countess Margaret was also a great friend of Mary's mother, Queen Katharine. The two women sometimes daydreamed as mothers will. Perhaps one day, the mothers said, Mary would wed the countess's son Reginald Pole. But Henry had other marriage schemes in mind, as we have seen, and nothing came of these daydreams. Nevertheless, Reginald Pole did play an important part in Mary's later life.

The year 1525 saw a major change for nine-year-old Mary. King Henry decided it was time to give her the title Princess of Wales. This was—and still is—the traditional title for the heir to the British throne. It was an important acknowledgment that Mary was Henry's only heir and would presumably inherit the crown. With the new title, Henry also increased the size of her household and sent her to live on the Welsh-English border.

In those days, a royal household included enough people to make a small village. Mary had her lady governess, twelve ladies in waiting, a chamberlain, a vice-chamberlain, a physician, an apothecary (who mixed the medicines), two chaplains, a dean of the chapel, a cupbearer, a carver (to cut up the meat), eight gentlemen waiters, a clerk of the jewel house, a minstrel, two messengers, fourteen yeomen of the bedchamber, one laundress (*she* must have been busy) and assorted other household members for a total of 81 individuals.

But these were only the "important" people. Though some of their titles were not very high-sounding, most of the persons just named had their own staff as well. The Countess of Salisbury had ten personal servants. The chamberlain (whose duty was to manage the household business) had eight. Even Mary's tutor, Master Fetherstone, had three. And each of the twelve ladies in waiting had two servants of her own. When all the servants were added, they brought the total in Mary's household to 194 people. And the lists do not mention any cooks or stable hands, so we must assume even more people were to be hired locally once Mary arrived in Wales.

So Mary rode west in a procession that included dozens of carts to carry all the clothing, feather beds, kettles, dishes, musical instruments, and other possessions of herself and her new court. Mary's wagons also carried along some 1,600 yards of blue and green cloth (Mary's personal colors) to be made into uniforms for her servants. Then there were the chapel furnishings—prayer stools, mass books, and candlesticks. And, of course, tapestries for the walls of her new home.

Tapestries (large embroidered or woven wall hangings) were more than decorations. Hung on the cold stone walls of rooms in castles or manor houses, they helped to keep out the chill. In general, those rooms would have seemed very bare to us. The only items of furniture were clothing chests and wardrobes, a few beds, and some stools and benches. There were no sofas, upholstered chairs, end tables, or chests of drawers, as all of these came into use much later.

One important item that definitely did travel with Mary was a little "chair of state" with a cloth-of-gold canopy. The princess sat in this chair in her great hall on public occasions. Just sitting in a chair marked her as the most important person in the room, because chairs were scarce and reserved for the high and mighty.

Ludlow Castle, now in ruins, was Mary's headquarters while in Wales. Life in such a place may appear romantic until one imagines its dark, drafty walls during a wet Welsh winter.
(*The Shropshire Gazeteer*, 1824)

On her journey to Ludlow Castle, where she would make her head-quarters for the next year and a half, Mary was accompanied not only by her household, but by her own Council. As Princess of Wales she needed a council, or group of advisers, to carry out her public duties. Council members and their servants added another 55 persons to the party.

The Council had the power to act for the king in certain matters, such as settling legal disputes and seeing that the king's laws were obeyed. Though Mary was too young to attend the Council's meetings, she still played a part in government. It was important that the people along the Welsh border should see their princess when she rode out hunting or hawking or when she passed through the little villages with their thatched or slate-roofed cottages. Just by her presence, Mary reminded the people of King Henry's power. When her officials settled a local quarrel, people understood that though the king might be far away, he had not forgotten their welfare.

When not traveling, Mary spent her time like any noble young lady—in study, prayer, music, dancing, needlework, and hunting. Especially important were Latin and French, in both of which she made excellent progress. Her French tutor was an amiable man who joked that French seemed unknown in Wales except in his own classroom.

Mary's later life shows she enjoyed games, many of which she probably learned about this time. Lawn bowls, as the name suggests, was an outdoor game similar to bowling. There were dozens of card games, with names like Primero, All Fours, Gleek, and Trump. Games with cards and dice were a good way to have fun in cold and rainy weather, of which England and Wales had plenty.

But even as Mary grew from a child to a young teenager in the sudden hills and green valleys of Wales, affairs were building to a crisis that would shatter her world. Soon events would force her to choose between her father and her mother.

Henry the king was a man of great talents and great flaws. He raised England from a second-rate nation off the coast of France to a power that could hold its own against the other great states of Europe. But Henry could be selfish and a bit of a bully. He expected to get whatever he wanted. And the one particular thing he wanted that life had failed to give him was a son.

By 1527, Henry had been married to Katharine of Aragon for seventeen years, during which time they appeared to be a loving couple. But the marriage of Henry and Katharine had a story behind it, and that story would soon become the talk of all Europe. Though Mary certainly knew the facts of the story, she had no idea how completely it was about to change her life. The first sign of the change came when King Henry ordered the princess to return from Wales.

Chapter 2

Princess No More

*T*he decision to bring the princess and her little court home from Wales resulted partly from Welsh resentment of English taxes. What if there were a rebellion, with the princess held as a hostage? A second reason why Mary came home in the early part of 1527 was that Henry was considering yet another marriage for her. This time the proposed bridegroom was France's king, Francis I, a man nearly her father's age, and Henry's dearest enemy and rival. The French had sent over a team of representatives to negotiate the terms of the proposed marriage, and as usual, lavish entertainment was provided for the visitors.

On one particular day at court, eleven-year-old Mary herself was the star of the occasion. She sat at her own table for the banquet, surrounded by the French envoys and ladies of the court. Viols and sackbuts (a form of trombone) provided sweet music while course after course was carried into the great hall, all served from dishes of gold plate and silver gilt. (The guests ate all this food with their fingers and table knives. Forks were a recent Italian fashion, not yet popular in England.)

Mary knew the importance of the occasion, for she had rehearsed her role long and hard, and spent many hours being fitted for her costume. Shortly after the banquet, all the guests were brought into the "disguising house" where the performance was to take place. First there was singing by the children of the king's chapel, followed by a mock debate and battle over the question of which was more valuable, love or riches. Finally, a curtain was pulled aside to reveal a cave constructed of cloth-of-gold, inside an artificial mountain decorated with coral, crystal, and "rich rocks of ruby." Then entered eight gentlemen in gold doublets and plumed helmets. By the light of the torches they carried, the audience could see eight maidens seated within the cave. They were dressed in cloth-of-gold with red tinsel, with garlands of jewels on their heads, and their hair caught back in nets of gold. Mary then rose and led the maidens down from the cave to perform a graceful and complicated dance. The Venetian ambassador wrote that Mary "dazzled the sight in such wise as to make one believe that she was decked with all the gems of the eighth [heavenly] sphere." By the time her father and several other noblemen came in, disguised, to join the dancing, most young girls would have been floating as high as the royal banners that flew above the castle.

The celebration lasted until the early hours of that May morning. At the very end, the king, in the role of proud father, brought Mary over to the French envoys and carefully loosed the jeweled net, letting the princess's heavy red-gold hair spill over her shoulders. Beautiful, beloved, and accomplished, Mary was the picture of a true princess on that night.

But Henry was a great one for achieving several purposes at once, and there was a less pleasant reason why he wanted Mary at court just then. In 1527, Henry was thinking of ending his marriage to Queen Katharine.

The king's desire for a son was well known. So was his passion for the lively, entrancing, and firmly unavailable Mistress Ann Boleyn. Ann had recently returned from the French court to serve as one of Katharine's ladies in waiting.

In her mid-twenties, Ann seemed well able to give Henry a son. But she insisted that any child of hers must be born in wedlock (which was what the king needed in any case). Encouraged by Cardinal Wolsey, who never let human decency stand in the way of his service to his royal master, Henry got the idea that the pope in Rome would easily understand his need for a male heir and agree to annul the marriage to Katharine.

An annulment would mean the marriage had been illegal from the first. Henry thought the queen herself might even show her loyalty by agreeing to retire to a community of nuns.

Henry was remembering the nearly forgotten fact that in 1501 Katharine had actually been married to his older brother Arthur. The marriage lasted only a short time, since Arthur died in 1502. But in the Bible's Book of Leviticus, Chapter 20, verse 21, Henry found a text that confirmed his worst fears. "If a man takes his brother's wife, it is impurity...They shall be childless." Perhaps this was the problem, Henry thought, even though the pope had given special permission for him to marry his brother's widow.

Henry's concern may have been just a convenient excuse, a real matter of conscience, or a combination of the two. With a man as self-centered and complex as Henry, motives are always hard to unravel. In any case, the year 1527 marked the beginning of a sad and trying period for Mary. In July, Henry asked Katharine directly for an annulment, stressing his pangs of guilt over breaking God's law. Katharine responded that she knew herself to be Henry's true and lawful wife, and that she would remain so until death. For the rest of her life, she never wavered from this position, and she encouraged Mary to take the same stand. Mary did, but at a terrible cost.

Henry now did what all-too-many discontented parents do—he used his child as a tool in the dispute over ending his marriage. First came persuasion, then threats, then banishment from court, and finally and most cruelly, forced separation of mother and daughter. But Mary also held firm, supporting her mother fully. In this, she was a lot more like Henry himself than he would have cared to admit. As a family, the Tudors were exceptionally strong willed.

For the next six years, Henry pursued his annulment like a huntsman after a king stag, with the prize always just out of reach. Finally, Katharine and Henry both appeared before a court composed of Church officials. It was a dramatic scene. First, Katharine threw herself at

Henry's feet, declaring that she loved him and was his true wife before God. When that failed, Katharine appealed her case directly to the pope, where she knew she was very likely to win. Then she walked out on the proceedings, a rather plump, aging queen with nothing but her dignity.

Prince Arthur, King Henry's older brother and Queen Katharine's first husband, about 1502.
(A. F. Pollard, *Henry VIII*, 1902)

Henry was embarrassed, and when Henry was embarrassed, someone had to pay. In this case, it was Cardinal Wolsey. Wolsey had been the most powerful man in the kingdom, next to Henry. Now, Wolsey was noisily and publicly dismissed from his office as chancellor. Then Henry had him arrested. The Cardinal was on his way to prison in the Tower of London when he fell ill and died. But the affair of the annulment, now known to all as "the king's great matter," dragged on and on.

In the first years of this turmoil, Mary was reasonably well off. Her mother was still living at court, though Henry was often seen in public with Ann Boleyn. Yet there is very little information about the princess in court records. It is as if she were a set of embroidered linens, folded away in a chest until needed.

Thomas, Cardinal Wolsey, Lord Chancellor. Wolsey failed to secure Henry VIII a divorce from Queen Katharine, lost favor with the king and fell from power.
(A.F. Pollard, *Henry VIII*, 1902)

Mary did spend Christmas of 1529 at court and her father gave her a New Year's present of 20 pounds (English money) with the instruction to amuse herself. Mary was now in her early teens and contracted to marry, not France's King Francis I, but his second son the Duke d'Orleans. In the marriage game, that showed how many points Mary had lost. Still, Henry continued to pay for her clothes, a wardrobe fit for a princess. At age fifteen, Mary received not only gowns of purple and black velvet, crimson satin, and silver tissue, but sixteen pairs of velvet shoes and a large supply of French hoods, Spanish gloves, fine cloth for smocks, and ribbons for trimming. As to what she was doing, an envoy from the Italian city of Milan reported at this time that she was occupied with "very becoming studies," and was "already advanced in wisdom and stature." In other words, Mary was still treated like a princess, but at the same time she was made to witness the increasingly bitter struggle between the now dowdy queen and her glamorous, black-eyed rival Ann Boleyn.

Aside from the tension between Katharine and Ann, the major cloud on Mary's horizon was the beginning of some sort of menstrual problem that would continue to bother her all her life. There is not enough information for modern doctors to diagnose the difficulty, but Mary seems to have had extremely severe cramps and other symptoms that would send her to bed almost every month. This became so routine that members of her household referred to it as "her usual illness."

Something worse than any cramps was ahead for Mary. In the summer of 1531, Henry became so angry with Katharine that he banished her from court and told her he didn't want to see her, ever again. Despite this breach, Mary was allowed to make a month-long visit to Katharine at Windsor, where the two enjoyed themselves by visiting several of the other royal residences in the neighborhood. They also spent much time in hunting. Mary had always loved the outdoors and the excitement of the chase, with its horns, its baying hounds, and the swift galloping after red deer, roe deer, hare, or fox.

Drawing of Windsor Castle, showing the country around it, where Mary and Queen Katharine enjoyed riding.
(A. F. Pollard, *Henry VIII,* 1902)

After Mary's visit with her mother, however, the two were treated all the more harshly. Katharine was ordered to travel to the More, a dank and old-fashioned residence well north of London, and Mary was sent to the Palace of Richmond. From now on, the king decreed, she was forbidden to see her mother. It was a hard, cruel thing to do to a fifteen-year-old girl, and Mary never got over it.

But if Henry thought he would destroy the mother-daughter relationship by forbidding Mary and Katharine to meet, he had forgotten his own boast, all those years ago. Mary was "the little girl who never cries." She and her mother exchanged letters regularly—letters carried in secret by loyal servants. In these letters, Katharine advised her daughter very specifically on matters of health, education, and politics. Above all, she wanted Mary to understand that Henry was the king, their dear husband and father, and was to be obeyed in all things except matters of conscience that no good Christian could ignore. Whatever Henry did or said to her, she returned him nothing but loving words.

As tactics to use against an all-powerful opponent, Katharine and Mary could hardly have chosen better. Nothing is more annoying than fighting with someone who won't fight back. Indeed, their actions were a version of what today would be called passive resistance, which was used successfully by both Mahatma Gandhi and Martin Luther King, Jr., in fighting against injustice. The behavior of his queen and his daughter infuriated Henry, but there was little he could do about it.

While Henry was occupied with ending his marriage, the courts and universities of Europe were filled with passionate arguments over religion. When Princess Mary was only a year old, a determined young monk named Martin Luther had set the debate aflame by marching up to the door of the cathedral in Wittenburg, Germany, and posting a list of 95 ways in which he disagreed with the practices of the Catholic Church. Henry had prided himself on supporting the Catholic Church against Luther. But now Henry wanted to be free of Katharine more than he wanted to be a true son of the Church. If the pope would not annul Henry's marriage, maybe Henry would simply reject the pope's authority altogether. And in Henry's court there were many individuals (some sincere, some self-serving) who were anxious to influence him toward one religious view or another. The Boleyn family was one that favored some of the new things that were being discussed, such as printing the Bible in

English rather than Latin, a truly revolutionary idea at the time. (William Tyndale, who translated the Bible into English in 1526, was later executed for doing so.)

Watching from a distance, Katharine and Mary saw Henry set himself on a path that would end in a final break with the pope. The causes were Henry's passion for his new love Ann, his desire for a son, and his belief that whatever Henry wanted, God must also want. But Henry himself certainly never foresaw the long-term results of his actions.

At the same time, Katharine and Mary were not alone in opposing the king's views on the power of the pope. By far their most loyal and imaginative supporter was a young man who arrived in 1529 to serve as ambassador from Katharine's nephew Charles V, the Holy Roman Emperor. The young man's name was Eustace Chapuys, and he took very seriously his diplomatic instructions, which were to protect Katharine's and Mary's interests and break up the affair with Ann Boleyn if possible. Like a chivalrous knight in the popular romances about the court of King Arthur, he thought it was his duty to rescue two royal ladies from the clutches of an evil king.

In addition to Eustace Chapuys, Katharine and Mary had several allies at court. One was Henry's younger sister Mary, who was known as the Tudor Rose. This aunt of Princess Mary's had befriended the young Katharine of Aragon when she arrived at the English court all those years ago. Another ally was the saintly Bishop John Fisher. He joined Chapuys in urging Charles V to send an army to restore Katharine and Mary to their rightful places.

Still, from 1531 on, things grew steadily worse for the two women. Henry by now was trying to force them to acknowledge publicly that his marriage with Katharine had been illegal. The consequence of this idea was as clear as it was shocking. If Katharine and Henry had never been truly married, then Mary was a bastard, no better than her half brother Henry Fitzroy, the son of Bessie Blount.

Queen Katharine of Aragon in middle age.
(A. F. Pollard, *Henry VIII*, 1902)

At this time in history, the term *bastard* was commonly used. In certain circumstances, it was even honorable. For example, the plays of Shakespeare, written during the next century, contain characters forthrightly called the Bastard of Orleans (in *Henry VI, Part One*) and Philip the Bastard (in *King John*). But it was one thing to rise to power as the bastard child of a nobleman and a comparatively humble mother. It was quite another to suggest that a grandchild of reigning kings and queens on both sides should suddenly cease to be heir to the throne and become merely "the Lady Mary." Yet this was exactly what the king was now demanding—and he had what seemed to him the best of reasons.

In January 1533, Henry secretly married Ann, who had at last given in to her royal lover and was pregnant. In May, Henry persuaded Thomas Cranmer, Archbishop of Canterbury, to annul the marriage to Katharine on his own authority.

And so, on a Thursday at the end of May 1533, Ann had her moment of triumph. Glowing in cloth-of-gold, she rode upriver to the royal residence at the Tower of London, accompanied by over a hundred gilded and decorated barges, with musicians, a mechanical dragon snorting flames, banners, and so much cannon fire that nearby windows in the homes of rich foreigners shattered as loudly and completely as a thousand years of religious tradition. (The poorer folk had oiled paper or horn for their windows, which saved them from the effects of the cannon fire.) Then, on June 1, Ann was crowned queen of England. The only thing missing was a cheering crowd, for the Londoners still loved their little Spanish queen.

There was a humorous sidelight to this and to Henry's four later marriages. Every time there was a new queen, workmen and artists had to scurry around changing the royal initials that appeared everywhere, from embroidered cushions to stained glass in the churches, to stonework and woodwork in the royal palaces. Inevitably, they overlooked some sets of initials, and it became something of a game in later times to try to spot leftover examples of Henry and Katharine's HK, as opposed to Henry and Ann's HA. Many people said, although not in the king's hearing, that the H and A should be read as, "Ha, ha!"

Ann Boleyn, about 1532, a few months before her marriage to Henry. The king had been enamored of her for five years.

(A. F. Pollard, *Henry VIII*, 1902)

At the same time, Henry was taking a much harsher view of Katharine's refusal to agree that her marriage was illegal. He sent several nobles to inform her that her title was now Princess Dowager (that is, the widow of the dead prince Arthur). Katharine, even though she was in bed with an infected toe, told the men she would never accept such a title. Then, since they were supposed to make a written report to Henry of all she had said, she demanded to see the document and crossed out every reference to herself as princess dowager, replacing each one with "the Quene." The document still exists, scratched by her angry pen strokes.

In the outside world, there were individuals who dared speak up for Katharine just as bravely. One was Elizabeth Barton, known as "the Holy Maid of Kent." She was a nun in a convent at Canterbury, a small city south of London.

The Holy Maid had visions, which told her that Henry's affair with Ann was wrong and that God would punish him and England if he didn't return to Katharine. The fame of the Holy Maid shows how much the people worried about the plight of Katharine and Mary, whom many still regarded as their rightful queen and princess, no matter what the king might say.

At the same time, things were not going well between Henry and Ann. The king began paying attention to another lady of the court (whose name is not even recorded). When, in September 1533, Ann gave birth to a healthy girl child (named Elizabeth, after the king's mother), Henry made a brief attempt to seem pleased, but his real attitude was quite different. Henry felt cheated. Where was the son he so richly deserved? Furthermore, he felt he had been wronged, because Pope Clement had excommunicated him after hearing that he had married Ann.

Excommunication was the harshest punishment the Church could hand down. It was supposed to mean that the king could not hear mass, could not receive any of the sacraments of the Church, and would be damned forever when he died. Needless to say, Henry actually went right on attending church, served by his loyal bishops and priests. But he was furious that this awful thing had happened to him.

Chapter 3

No Way Out

At this point, Katharine and Mary began to see their situation as desperate. Ambassador Chapuys reported that in 1533 Queen Ann had boasted that she would make Mary serve as one of her maids, marry her to a nobody, or even "give her too much dinner," meaning poison her. (Chapuys's reports were often exaggerated, but if even part of this was true, it was alarming.) Later that year, Henry's chief adviser Thomas Cromwell demanded a list of all Mary's royal jewels so they could be taken away to the royal treasury as Katharine's had been. The unfortunate man who arrived to deliver this message had not reckoned with Mary's Lady Governess, Margaret Pole, the Countess of Salisbury. Outfaced and out-argued by this niece of two kings, he backed down completely and had to write to King Henry confessing total failure.

Then in October came the order that Mary was no longer to have her personal household, already reduced to about 162 persons. This new attack on her status included losing her dear Countess Margaret. The king ordered Mary to report to the household of the infant Princess Elizabeth, where she would become a simple waiting woman, losing the title of princess. Now Mary was not only the princess in the tower, she was Cinderella.

In December Thomas Howard, the Duke of Norfolk, arrived at Mary's manor with a group of his men and ordered Mary to prepare herself to leave immediately, taking only two of her women. The Countess of

Salisbury begged to go along, saying she would pay her own expenses, but Norfolk refused. He was, after all, Ann Boleyn's uncle—a cold, shrewd man with no sympathy for Mary, either personal or political. So off Mary went to Hatfield House, to serve the child she considered a bastard, in the same way that Ann's party considered Mary one.

At Hatfield, Mary lived a life that would have broken the nerve of many seventeen-year-olds. The other members of Elizabeth's household missed no chance to snub, tease, or mock her. There was almost no one she could trust except her two women and a groom or manservant of her mother's named Anthony Roke, who carried many forbidden messages between them. Thus worry, stress, loneliness, and a perfectly justifiable resentment were Mary's constant companions. It is no wonder that she was often ill during this period.

Mary's only comfort, she would recall later, was in her music and books. By now, she played several keyboard and stringed instruments, and there was plenty of music available, from lively dances to the laments of jilted lovers. Her reading included the newly rediscovered works of Greek and Roman poets, historians, and philosophers. Like her mother, Mary was a follower of the "New Learning," as this study of the classical world was called. Yet Mary was now so closely confined that she could not even enjoy her daily exercises of riding and walking. When she wrote to the king claiming her health was being affected, things got a little better, and she was again allowed to go out. Still, most of her clothes and jewels were taken away as punishment for her refusal to address Elizabeth as princess, or to allow others to address her as the Lady Mary. Also, she was still officially forbidden to write to her mother, although she continued to get news of Katharine by secret means. What she heard did nothing to cheer her.

The queen, now living in a manor house called Buckden, had confined herself to a single room. She was having her women cook all her food there because she feared she might be poisoned. Some historians have found this fear exaggerated, and certainly there is no evidence that any poison plot actually existed. At the same time, it was an age when poison was a weapon of state, especially in Italy. Then there was Queen Ann's threat against Mary, reported earlier. The threat was mentioned by Ambassador Chapuys in one of his letters to the emperor, and since he was one of Katharine's most trusted friends, she probably heard the story from him and believed it, whether or not it was true. Katharine became anxious about Mary's safety as well as her own.

Over time, Queen Ann's attitude to Katharine and Mary had grown even more hostile. Frightened and insecure after the birth of Elizabeth, Ann even claimed she would not be able to become pregnant again as long as Katharine and Mary still lived. She urged Henry to put them to death so that the party of "the Old Religion" (the Catholics) could not use them as a rallying point for rebellion.

For Mary, perhaps the very worst moment of this wretched time came when Elizabeth's household was moved from Hatfield in March 1534. As usual, Mary protested against the fact that this upstart baby was being treated as a princess, while she was expected to travel as an ordinary waiting woman. She stated that she would rather remain behind than go under such conditions. Then "certain gentlemen" took hold of her and forced her into the traveling litter that was carrying Elizabeth's governess, Lady Shelton. To lay hands on a royal person was very close to treason. That these men dared to treat Mary so roughly underlined the low state to which she had fallen.

A different sort of pretty eighteen-year-old might have been quick to lighten her life by starting a love affair. However, Mary knew that any hint of scandal would be used against her and, worse, against Katharine. On the other hand, Mary may have had fewer romantic opportunities than one might think. Any young man in Elizabeth's household who tried to flirt with or even be kind to Mary was likely to be punished or dismissed.

Henry's own treatment of his daughter was extremely painful to her. On more than one occasion, he came to visit Elizabeth but ordered that Mary be locked in her room while he was there. Even so, Mary still felt love for her father and believed, as Katharine did, that all his actions were the fault of evil advisers. And the king's fatherly feeling for Mary cannot have been entirely gone, for once, when discussing her with the French ambassador, his eyes filled with tears at mention of her good breeding and virtue.

But Henry had a great deal on his mind at this time, other than Mary. First of all, Ann was pregnant again early in 1534, but she gave birth to a stillborn child. This weakened Ann's position and increased Henry's anxiety about fathering a son. Now in his forties, he was not only growing stout and bald, he had a painful ulcer on his leg that would not heal. Like many athletic people, he resented illness of any sort and was a very irritable patient. In addition, Henry was no fool. He knew as well as anyone that his people were more and more unhappy with his new marriage, his break with the Catholic Church, and his treatment of Katharine and Mary. He feared a rebellion, an act of treason, even a foreign invasion. It seemed to him that both his first wife and his elder daughter were a threat to his power.

Then, in February 1535, Mary suffered a really severe illness. She was so sick that some feared (and others hoped) that she might die. The one thing Mary longed for in her misery was to be allowed to see her mother. Under Katharine's care, and that of her personal physician, Mary was sure she would get better. A request was sent to the king, and then Henry did a truly unkind thing. He ruled that Mary could be moved to a place *near* her mother, but could not actually see her. Doubtless he saw this as generous, but there was cruelty hidden beneath the generosity. The only satisfaction either Mary or Katharine got was to have the queen's physician visit Mary and carry messages between them, knowing that a short ride was all that separated them. And though neither of them knew it, this was to be Mary's last chance to see her mother alive.

Mary did recover, and when she did, there were two major things on her mind. One was the shocking executions Henry ordered in that year—executions of Catholics whose only crime was that they refused to take the Oath of Supremacy, which named the king as head of the English Church. First came the deaths of four monks who were hanged, disemboweled, and beheaded as if they had been common criminals. To make sure the people knew how heartily he approved of these terrible deaths, Henry sent both the Duke of Norfolk and Henry Fitzroy as witnesses. Shortly afterward, three other monks were similarly executed, after enduring seventeen days of the worst sort of imprisonment, chained upright to the wall of their dungeon.

Sir Thomas More (left), Lord Chancellor and man of principle, paid with his head for his opposition to Henry's divorce from Katharine and the king's split from the Roman Catholic Church. Thomas Cromwell, the royal secretary, was a hard man despite the pious Latin inscription over his head. After More's fall, Cromwell became Henry's most influential adviser—until his turn came to lose his head.

(A. F. Pollard, *Henry VIII*, 1902)

Next came the death of Bishop John Fisher, the honorable churchman famed for his self-denial. Fisher was beheaded on Tower Hill for the crime of treason in not signing the oath. Little did Henry know that Fisher was in fact guilty of a different treason—writing to the emperor and urging him to invade England, rescue Katharine and Mary, and restore the kingdom to the Catholic Church. Ambassador Chapuys and others had been doing the same thing for years, but they were not Henry's subjects. Legally, it was certainly treason for an English subject like Fisher to call for a foreign invasion, in spite of the fact that Fisher himself saw his duty to God as higher than his duty to his king.

The last execution of 1535 was just as alarming. The former Lord Chancellor, Sir Thomas More, was a famed scholar, author, and statesman with learned friends all over Europe. That King Henry would execute this talented and charming man, one of his oldest friends, is evidence of the frightening climate of the times. Thomas More went to his death declaring that he was "the king's good servant, but God's first." Mary and Katharine had taken exactly the same position on many occasions

The site in the courtyard of the Tower of London where Sir Thomas More and later Ann Boleyn, Kathryn Howard, Thomas Cromwell, and many others were executed.

(*Pictorial London,* 1906)

When the monks were executed, Elizabeth's governess Lady Shelton had sternly warned Mary to mend her ways or follow in their footsteps. But though Mary was certainly miserable as a member of baby Elizabeth's household, she was not entirely helpless. The second thing on Mary's mind at this time was an escape from England. It seems to have been her first independent decision as an adult. She wanted to get out of her present situation, by whatever means possible. No matter how much her mother advised passive resistance, Mary was ready for more direct action. Without telling her mother, she was going to let their dear friend Ambassador Chapuys help her leave the country.

By April 1535, Chapuys was hatching a plan in which horsemen would snatch Mary up while she was out walking near her current residence, Eltham House in Kent. They would ride like the wind to the Thames River, only five miles away. There, she would board a waiting ship bound for some port in the Holy Roman Emperor's territory of the Netherlands (Flanders), right across the English Channel.

Fortunately for Mary, a prisoner with a daring escape plan is much happier than a prisoner without hope. Chapuys thought the easiest part of the plan would be finding a ship. Spanish and Flemish vessels frequently anchored in the Thames, and the ambassador was sure the country people would look the other way as the princess rode by. Meanwhile, with her heart in her throat, Mary had to carry on as usual. It was a task for someone of "great prudence and courage," as Chapuys said, but he knew he could count on her.

Mary had now made a decision that would stay with her all her life. She would no longer be a pawn or a martyr. Against all efforts to make her feel helpless and useless, she had developed a sense of her own destiny and purpose.

There were problems, however. Eustace Chapuys was more at home hatching plots than carrying them out. Scheme as he might, there never seemed to be just the right combination of armed men, ships, and cross-channel winds. Besides, Chapuys' master the Emperor Charles V had not quite, not exactly, not definitely told him to go ahead with the plan. Charles, in fact, had little interest in Katharine and Mary, unless their lives were directly threatened.

Later in the fall of 1535, Ambassador Chapuys received a mysterious visitor at his lodging. Heavily cloaked to hide her identity, this person turned out to be Gertrude, Marchioness of Exeter. Gertrude and her husband the Marquess had always been among Mary and Katharine's supporters. (Gertrude's mother had been one of Queen Katharine's Spanish waiting women.) Now Gertrude had alarming news for the ambassador. Through highly placed friends, the couple had heard that Henry had angrily told his Council that the queen and princess must be condemned for treason at the next session of Parliament. Then, said the marchioness, when the king noticed that some of his Councilors were weeping at the thought of executing two such royal ladies, Henry declared that neither tears nor "wry faces" would change his mind.

This tale, brought to Chapuys by a woman who was risking her life to do it, at last drove Charles V to action. Finally, the emperor instructed his captain general in the Netherlands, the Count de Roeulx, to send his best man to England in a daring attempt to bring Mary to safety.

De Roeulx's agent did indeed come to England, very early in 1536. This man, whose name is still unknown (he was a *really* secret agent), quickly set forth a plan that would have Mary in the Netherlands by February. Then, losing no time, lords who were fed up with Henry would begin a rebellion in her name in March or April. If all went well, Henry would be out of a throne, and perhaps out of this world, by May.

Thus began Mary's twentieth year, 1536—a year of turmoil, tragedy, and startling events.

Chapter 4

The Wheel of Fortune

At Kimbolton Manor, Queen Katharine was dying. She had been in poor health for some time, weighed down by grief, worry, and a peculiar form of guilt. Katharine, whom many regarded as a near saint, was tortured by the idea that if she had given in to Henry and quietly entered a convent, the realm of England might not have fallen into heresy (false religion).

In the first week of January 1536, Katharine was able to receive a final visit from Eustace Chapuys. The ambassador stayed at Kimbolton for four days, speaking at length with Katharine and recording her last messages. The room was always full of physicians, servants, officials, and even a spy sent by Thomas Cromwell, the king's chief adviser, so the two old friends could not speak freely. Nevertheless, the ambassador answered all Katharine's many questions about Henry's health and dealings with other rulers, as well as her concerns for her much-loved Mary. Chapuys did his best to comfort her, saying that God was using the rise of Protestantism (as the reformed religion had come to be called) to test people's faith and that she should not blame herself for the break with the pope. The presence of her old ally seemed to strengthen Katharine considerably, and one of the ambassador's men even entertained her by telling jokes. Chapuys left, thinking to return if Katharine grew worse again. He never made it back.

But Katharine was to have another beloved visitor before the end. One of her dear friends was a former lady in waiting, Maria de Salinas, now Lady Willoughby. Hearing of Katharine's illness, this courageous woman ordered her horse saddled and rode sixty wintry miles alone through the night to reach Kimbolton. She had come once before and been turned away. This time, Maria would hear no arguments, but went straight to the queen's room and locked the door behind her.

On January 7, it was clear to everyone that Katharine was in her final hours. She heard mass and received the last rites of the Church, but she was not legally able to make a will since, in her own eyes at least, she was a married woman, and married women could not leave property. She did, however, dictate a letter to King Henry, asking him to fulfill her dying wishes. Such little money as she had, she hoped he would give to her loyal servants, and add to it a year's wages. She requested masses for her soul and asked that someone would make a pilgrimage on her behalf to the shrine of Our Lady of Walsingham. She had little to leave to Mary except some furs and a gold collar that she had brought with her from Spain more than thirty years before. Her more lasting legacy to her daughter was the support and loyalty of the English Catholics.

Touchingly, Katharine's last messages to Henry were loving. She said she forgave him for everything and hoped he would be a kind father to Mary. She prayed he would take thought for his soul's salvation. The letter closed like this: "Lastly, I make this vow, that mine eyes desire you above all things." After that, Katharine prayed for her husband and daughter. She died about two in the afternoon, in the arms of Maria de Salinas. Needless to say, Mary was not present, nor had Katharine ever dared hope that she would be. It is strange to think that with Katharine's death, Henry may have lost the only one of his wives who truly loved him.

As soon as Katharine died, rumors began to suggest she had been poisoned. For this reason, one of the castle's tradesmen was called in to cut open her body. (Physicians of those days did not do autopsies.) When the man cut open Katharine's heart, he found a hideous black growth on it.

Katharine had died, appropriately enough, of cancer of the heart. But the doctors who were present thought the signs might point to slow poison.

Yet it was not Katharine who died of poison, but her great rival Ann Boleyn. Within the next few months, Ann was poisoned, though not by arsenic or henbane. What would kill Queen Ann was the poison of envy and gossip, along with a tidy little plot worked out by Henry's conniving secretary, Thomas Cromwell.

When news of Katharine's death reached the royal court, Henry celebrated by dressing himself in yellow and putting a white feather in his hat. He carried two-year-old Elizabeth to mass in his arms, had his midday dinner, and followed the meal by dancing with the ladies of the court. Then he went out to the tiltyard, mounted his horse, and broke many lances in mock combat, showing more energy than he had for some time. If he also wept when he read Katharine's last letter, as one report suggests, we should not be surprised, knowing Henry. He was a man of contradictory emotions.

Meanwhile, Mary had been informed of her mother's death by Lady Shelton (in a very abrupt and heartless manner). Chapuys feared Mary might not be able to bear the news because she "loved and cherished [her mother] as much, and perhaps more than any daughter ever did." But Mary somehow conquered her grief, at least in public. Her first request was that Katharine's physician and apothecary be sent to her, but this was not because she was ill. It was a pretext designed to gain first-hand reports of her mother's last hours, which she probably could not have had in any other way.

Less than three weeks later, there was more news for Mary, though certainly no one brought it to her officially. Queen Ann had again given birth—to a second stillborn child, this one a boy.

Within a month of Katharine's death, Mary's escape plan was getting in gear again. But suddenly little Elizabeth's household was moved to Hunsdon, which was forty miles from the Thames River, not five. Now there would have to be relays of horses and a sizable armed guard to lead the escape party through some large towns. On the positive side, Mary thought her guards had become less watchful recently. Perhaps they saw as clearly as anyone else that Queen Ann's star was setting. Mary hoped to give her ladies a sleeping potion and then sneak out of the house to join her mounted rescuers. But the chances of discovery were now much greater, and Chapuys advised delay, at least until after Easter.

Queen Ann knew very well how dangerous her situation was. With Katharine dead and herself apparently unable to bear a male child, Henry was (at least from the Catholic point of view) free to marry again, since his marriage to Ann had never been lawful in the first place. Furthermore, since the middle of the previous year, Henry had been casting romantic looks at a young woman named Jane Seymour, one of Queen Ann's ladies.

At this moment, Thomas Cromwell took up the challenge of getting rid of Ann. The clergy had already tried and failed to find some reason to annul the marriage. Cromwell thought an accusation of treason would do just as well. With his usual energy and thoroughness, Cromwell began first to look for and then to invent evidence against Henry's second, now-unwanted queen.

Ann was arrested on May 1, 1536, after watching a May Day tournament with the king. She was taken to the Tower of London, which served both as royal residence and as prison. Her "trial" took place on May 15, before a court that included her uncle the Duke of Norfolk. This jury was not looking for the truth, it was doing the king's dirty work for him. Ann was condemned to die, either by burning or by beheading, "at the king's pleasure." No voice was raised in her defense, not even her own father's. Both Norfolk and Sir Thomas Boleyn could see which way the wind was blowing, and that wind was filling the sails of the Seymour family. Boleyn and Norfolk were afraid for their own careers, if not their lives, but that was no excuse.

On May 19, Ann walked the short distance to the Tower Green, mounted the wooden platform, knelt at the block, and had her head struck off by a skilled French executioner brought over from Calais for the occasion. The next day, Henry went through a betrothal ceremony with Jane Seymour.

Now both Mary and three-year-old Elizabeth were motherless. Furthermore, both were to be considered bastards, since Archbishop Cranmer lost no time in annulling Ann's marriage as well.

The sudden, unforeseen fall of Ann Boleyn left Mary and her supporters somewhat adrift. The plot for Mary's escape was still alive and well, but the situation had altered dramatically. The young woman Henry had chosen as his next bride, who was only about seven years older than Mary herself, was from a much more traditional family than the Protestant-leaning Boleyns. Perhaps it would be well to wait and see what sort of changes came to the court, now that the hated Ann was gone.

Historians in general have been very kind to Jane Seymour. Just as Katharine has been seen as the abandoned wife and Ann as the temptress, Jane has been the good woman, the mother, the sweet one. There is no doubt that Jane had positive qualities, among them her serious effort to be kind to Mary. She was also under great pressure from her ambitious family. But today we have to ask, how virtuous is it *really* to flirt with and accept gifts from a married king while his wife is first pregnant and then on trial for her life? And what about marrying the man less than two weeks after the previous wife's execution? Many people would say this was a little hasty.

Perhaps what attracted Henry was the simple fact that Jane was so very different from Ann. No temper here, no French glamour, no irresistible charm. Instead, the little we can gather about Jane from her history suggests she was conventional, cautious, and just a bit dull.

The one certain thing about Jane is that she served the interests of her two brothers, Edward ("Ned") and Thomas Seymour. The Seymours were definitely on their way up in 1536. Edward Seymour at this time was a successful military commander, a serious and practical man. His younger brother Tom was very different. He had a wild streak, an eye for the ladies, and a love of horseplay not unlike that of the young Henry Tudor.

As a family, the Seymours were quite conservative in their religious views, much more favorable to the Holy Roman Empire, and thus to Princess Mary, than the Boleyns had been. Almost as soon as Ann was dead, Jane began urging Henry to bring the disgraced princess back to court. Mary wrote her father a series of humble letters. She congratulated him on his marriage and said she hoped Jane would bear him healthy sons. She also begged to be restored to his good graces "in all matters saving my conscience." Yet Henry was not going to give an inch. He knew very well what Mary meant by her conscience. He sent another group of his Councilors, including the dukes of Norfolk and Sussex, to see her at Hunsdon. They demanded she sign the Oath of Supremacy, admitting that the king was head of the English Church and that Katharine's marriage had been illegal.

There was an ugly scene. The twenty-year-old princess defied the men who had come to frighten her into signing, and the meeting ended in a shouting match. One of the Councilors even said that if she had been his daughter, he would have had her beaten to death. (Parents had this right in Tudor times, horrible though it sounds.) Then the Councilors left. They told Lady Shelton (who was now Mary's governess) not to allow the princess to speak to anyone and to keep a close watch on her. The sharp-tongued Lady Shelton, who had never liked Mary, was only too happy to comply.

Indeed, Mary's situation was now very serious. Henry had executed Thomas More and Bishop Fisher for exactly the same "matter of conscience" that was bothering her. Now, when he heard of Mary's response to the Councilors, the king flew into a rage. He took the first steps toward having Mary tried for treason. What was Mary to do?

Ambassador Chapuys had often praised her for holding fast, but this time his advice was different. He pointed out to Mary that in the eyes of all right-thinking people, she was the heir to the English throne. He urged her to consider that she had a duty to preserve her own life. She had survived so far, he suggested, because she was to serve some higher purpose. And he reminded her that both the Catholic Church and English law held that a person was not bound by an oath taken under threat of force.

Mary considered. She no longer had her mother's reputation to defend. She was entirely on her own, worn down by years of scorn, loneliness, and dark hints about her future. The only thing that saved her was that the judges appointed to try her were unhappy about spilling royal blood. They gave her one last chance to obey, and this time Mary signed the statement. But clearly she signed with private reservations. She even asked Chapuys to write to the pope, asking him to pardon her for the sin of making a false statement. The incident was part of a hard lesson—at the court of *Henry VIII*, one could not afford to be too open. Discretion was useful, and silence could save your life.

In winning her way back into Henry's affections, Mary had had help from a surprising source. Thomas Cromwell, who had recently called Mary "the most obstinate woman that ever was," made it his business to support her return to court. Perhaps he remembered the time, years before, when he had said of Katharine's insistence that her marriage was legal, "But for her sex, she would have surpassed all the heroes of history." Tudor society had a very hard time dealing with women who did not crumple in the face of opposition. People tended to think that a woman with a mind of her own was acting like a man, or else was a "freak of nature."

Nevertheless, Cromwell was a realist, and there is a certain amount of admiration concealed in his remarks on both Katharine and Mary. The seventeen-year-old Henry Fitzroy (who was best known for playing hooky from his Latin studies to go hunting) was by now dead, a victim of tuberculosis like Henry's brother Arthur. Cromwell saw clearly that the king had no son and Mary was his eldest child, regardless of whether or not she was a bastard.

King Henry VIII, in about 1543, from a painting by Henry's favorite court artist, Hans Holbein.

(A. F. Pollard, *Henry VIII*, 1902)

To be fair to Henry, he was quite kind to Mary once she had given in and signed the letter he wanted. First he ordered her household to be restored. Immediately, there were many applications from people who had served her before she was sent to away Hatfield. Some of these individuals had been in her household from the time she was named Princess of Wales at the age of nine until it was disbanded. One was a waiting woman named Susan Clarencieux, who had been with Mary since the princess was a child and would remain with her till the day she died. Finally, about this time, Mary's household was brightened by the presence of Jane the Fool. Today, Jane would be a stand-up comic. Like all court fools, she had a duty to amuse her patron and guests with silly songs, riddles, pranks, and mocking comments on the blind spots and follies of the great. She stayed with Mary for many years, a trusted and valued servant.

In late summer 1536, Mary moved from Hunsdon to a house much nearer the court, where Henry and Jane rode out to meet her. Her father had not seen Mary since she was fifteen. In the leafy green of the English summer afternoon, the three spent several hours together in private. Having won his contest with Mary, Henry was in a generous and even loving mood. He gave Mary a thousand crowns in money and promised more to come. He also said he regretted their long separation (as if it had been someone else's fault). Mary said all the right things, but there was much that both she and her father were holding back. Queen Jane was less restrained. She made Mary a present of a valuable diamond ring and spoke warmly of the princess's future return to court.

Mary then went back to Hunsdon to complete her preparations and gather her household. She was now receiving much respect and many messages of friendship. Edward Seymour, who had become the king's lord chamberlain, invited her to ask for whatever she needed in the way of clothing. The jewels and clothes that had been taken from her as punishment while she served in little Elizabeth's household were returned. Cromwell sent her a fine-looking horse and saddle as a present. Evidently he knew about Mary's love of horseback riding.

Mary did indeed return to court, with all its entertainments. Although she was still officially a bastard, no one treated her that way. She was now the second lady of the land, following the queen at all state occasions and even sitting opposite her at table. Yet Mary still had to play something of a double game. For example, King Henry ordered her to send letters to the pope (now Paul III) and to her relatives Charles V and his half-sister Mary, Regent of the Netherlands, saying that she had completely changed her mind about the English Church and now accepted that her mother's marriage had been illegal. When she was younger, Mary would have refused and gotten herself into serious, perhaps fatal, trouble. The older and wiser Mary wrote the letters, smiled sweetly, and then instructed the faithful Ambassador Chapuys to warn his master that the letters were "not worth a straw," to use one of her favorite expressions.

Fortunately, Henry's mind was busy with other matters. This was the period when the king, with the enthusiastic help of Cromwell, began to shut down and destroy the 8,000 communities of monks and nuns that had been a part of English life for more than a thousand years. One of his motives was religious reform, but another was money. Henry made himself and his government enormously rich by taking the buildings, farms, golden crosses, breweries, coal fields, communion chalices, windmills, and jeweled altar furnishings that had once belonged to the monasteries. Many a former abbey or priory was handed over to a courtier as a reward for service to the king. Some wealthy families enriched the royal treasury by buying properties from the crown. One man who was thought worthy to receive a piece of Church land was a wool merchant named Lawrence de Wessington—a direct ancestor of George Washington.

The seizure of the monasteries was exactly what the English Catholics had feared most. For some, particularly in the northern parts of the country, it was the last straw. Now there was actually of the people in both Lincolnshire and Yorkshire.

rebellion had come two years earlier, it might have been the end for Mary. Now no one, not even the suspicious king, blamed the turmoil on her.

In the spring of 1537, Queen Jane announced that she was pregnant. Mary rejoiced along with everyone else. She had never expected to rule England. She only wanted her rightful place as Henry's eldest daughter. In October, at Hampton Court palace, Jane gave birth to a healthy son after fifty hours of difficult labor. The court was thrown into a whirlwind of both rejoicing and concern for the new prince's health. Fearful of disease as always, Henry ordered every inch of the baby's quarters to be scrubbed, swept, or polished, while no strangers were allowed inside the palace gates.

Mary was to have the honor of being the little prince's godmother. Wearing a new cloth-of-silver gown, Mary played her part in the hours-long christening ceremony and presented a gold cup as her christening gift. Then, as at her own christening 21 years before, a herald came forth to announce the baby's name and titles: "Edward, son and heir to the King of England, Duke of Cornwall and Earl of Chester." As they left the ceremony, Mary held her little sister Elizabeth by the hand. She had always loved children, and now that Henry's second daughter was also considered a bastard, it was almost possible for Mary to forget who the child's mother had been.

But all the concern for little Edward's health had been misplaced. It was Queen Jane who fell ill and died of "childbed fever" a few days after the christening.

Henry was deeply and sincerely grieved, but he was also terrified of death and everything to do with it. He rode away from the court as soon as he could, leaving Mary to take the sad and exhausting role of chief mourner. There were eighteen days of processions, masses, and vigils before Mary followed behind Jane's hearse to the queen's final resting place at Windsor.

King Henry VIII and his beloved son Prince Edward, from a carved onyx miniature.
(A.F. Pollard, *Henry VIII*, 1902)

Jane Seymour had been Henry's wife for less than two years. Her brothers were to remain in power for much, much longer.

Chapter 5

Stepmothers on Parade

*I*n the space of a mere year-and-a-half, Mary's fortunes had changed dramatically. Once friendless and virtually a prisoner, she was now the first lady in England. In the next several years, while her father renewed his search for the perfect wife, Mary was able to live a much more pleasant life. She spent time at Hampton Court, at the Palace of Richmond, and at various country manors in Kent and Surrey. Certainly she seems to have enjoyed her comparative independence.

As before, exercise, card playing, music, and reading (in French, Latin, and English) were among her private pleasures. She liked to take a two- or three-mile walk after breakfast, and she never went out without a purse full of small coins to give as charity. She had a special care for the former monks and nuns who had been made homeless by the closing of the monasteries. In addition, she still loved riding to the hunt and was especially fond of her pet Italian greyhounds.

While in the country, she took a keen interest in gardening. Wherever she went, she stayed in touch with a man named Jasper, who was head gardener at Beaulieu Manor, asking him to send her whatever was new and unusual in the plant world.

Mary liked children, as well as plants. She served as godmother at christenings and took joy in visiting the families of her many godchildren. She always brought suitable presents, often ordered from her personal goldsmith. Her country neighbors showed their gratitude by bringing her little gifts, such as quince pies and orange pies. (The latter were new and different, as it was barely ten years since the Portuguese had brought the first sweet oranges to Europe from Asia.)

When Mary was at court, she also showed a taste for fine clothes in rich colors such as crimson, purple, and gold. A noblewoman's clothing in Mary's time was complicated, and dressing required the help of maids or ladies in waiting. First came a linen or silk shift (something like a nightgown). The cuffs and standing collar of the shift would be beautifully embroidered. Women who wanted to control their figures could wear "body stitchets," which were like corsets, made with canvas, leather, or even iron. Mary certainly never needed body stitchets, as her figure was always referred to as thin or slight.

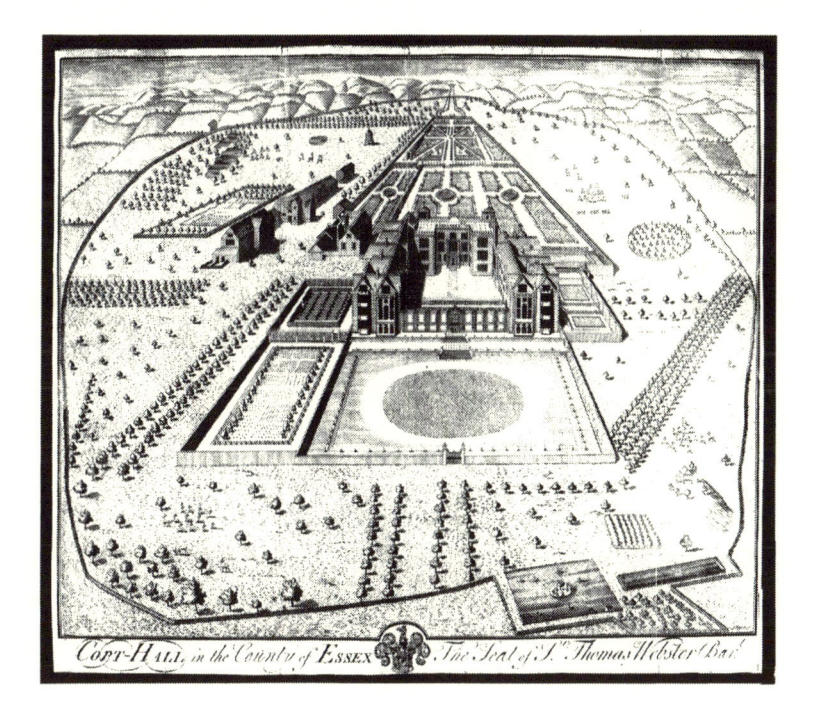

Copt Hall, a manor house in Essex, shows the formal style of Tudor gardens. Mary loved flowers and always took an interest in the gardens of her residences.

(By courtesy of the Essex Record Office)

Next came the sleeveless bodice in silk, damask, velvet, or another rich fabric. Black was one of the most popular colors, partly because black dye was the most expensive. Other colors had interesting names such as carnation, dove gray, lion tawny, willow green, russet, and bice (a pale blue). The bodice laced up the back, which was hard for a woman to do by herself. It was often joined to a second, triangular piece called the stomacher, which was rather like a wide belt. At this time (though not later in Mary's life), necklines were either high or square. The funnel-shaped or bell-shaped sleeves were a separate item, and were often a different color from the rest of the costume. The well-known song "Greensleeves" refers to this fashion. Sleeves had to be attached at the shoulder with pins, hooks, or ties, and the join was often hidden by rolls of cloth called wings. (Buttons had not been invented yet, except as decorations, and there were no sewn-in pockets.) The sleeves were often "slashed." This meant they had slits in them, through which the fabric of the shift was pulled out in a puff. The edges of the shift also showed at the cuffs and sometimes the neck. If the neckline was square, married women and modest maidens filled in the neck of the bodice with a separate piece of pleated or embroidered cloth called a partlet.

Below the waist, a woman wore a long skirt called a kirtle, which was usually open in front to show the "forepart," a heavily ornamented underskirt. Within a few years, a new garment known as the farthingale would be introduced from Spain. It was a bell-shaped version of the hoop skirt, designed to spread out the kirtle and emphasize the smallness of a woman's waist. Around the waist, many noblewomen wore a handsome chain of gold or beads, from which dangled a purse, a set of keys (if the lady was in charge of a great household), or a pomander (a pierced metal ball filled with something fragrant, such as an orange or apple stuck with cloves). Fragrance was a major concern because people didn't bathe very often (especially in winter), there was no indoor plumbing, and even the richest houses often stank of garbage. Every item that could possibly be perfumed was perfumed, including gloves.

On their heads, noblewomen wore the so-called French hood, a stiffened, rounded arch above the face, often embroidered with pearls or jewels. The background color was usually dark, and dark cloth hung down the back to cover all or most of the hair. Court ladies always wore jewels if they had them. By now, Mary had them. In addition to the jewels returned to her after Queen Ann's death, the princess had been given some of the fine pieces that once belonged to Queen Jane. Her jewelry was carefully listed in a "jewel book." Mary's attention to detail can be seen in her surviving signature on each page, showing she had checked the list and found it correct.

An example of Tudor jewel work. This figure of Saint George slaying the dragon is made of chased silver with rock crystal and colored gems. It may have been a gift from Henry VIII to the King of France.

(A. F. Pollard, *Henry VIII*, 1902)

When it came to Tudor jewelry, bigger was definitely better. Jeweled letters (monograms) were popular. Mary owned both an H for Henry and an M for Mary, which included many great stones such as rubies, pearls, and diamonds. Some pieces of jewelry were large enough to show complete biblical scenes, usually in colored enamels set in gold and surrounded with gems. Even allowing for the flattery so commonly offered to royalty, it is not hard to believe that the fair, slender Mary in her fine clothes and jewels was indeed "one of the belles of this court," as the French ambassador said in 1541. Poets and minstrels had begun calling her romantically "the marigold," punning on the name Mary and the color of her hair.

Another diplomat, this one a Spaniard, gave Mary a back-handed compliment that shows much about her, and much about the age she lived in. She had, he said, "very great goodness and discretion," as well as a praiseworthy skill in *hiding her accomplishments*. By this, he meant Mary's achievements in music and scholarship. She was not the first, nor the last, woman to find that in the eyes of the world it was a bad idea to be too smart or too talented.

What the diplomats thought of her may have been important to Mary because now, in her mid-twenties, her marriage was very much on her mind, and on King Henry's. The trouble was, no suitor seemed exactly right to Henry. In reality, Henry's main goal was to prevent France and the Habsburg Dominions from ganging up on him, and each of them had a similar concern about the other two. This made the *possible* marriage of Mary a more valuable diplomatic game piece than her *actual* marriage.

There was also Elizabeth to consider. She was no longer a motherless baby, but a sharp-eyed and very bright little girl who was already showing outstanding ability in her studies. Naturally, considering their ages, it was Mary who really wanted to wed at this point. But Mary found that the only man her real friends thought she should marry was exactly the last suitor Henry would accept.

For a decade at least, people had been talking about a match between the Countess of Salisbury's son Reginald Pole and Princess Mary. Reginald had royal Plantagenet blood from his mother, Mary's beloved Lady Governess. He was gentle and kind, and he had been extremely well educated in both England and Italy, which was the international center of art, literature, architecture, and philosophy at the time. Also, through a quirk of Catholic law, he was free to marry even though he was a cardinal.

But Thomas Cromwell was deeply suspicious of Reginald Pole and his entire family. From the safety of foreign parts, Cardinal Pole had repeatedly condemned Henry's closing of the monasteries, his claims to be head of the English Church, and his views on religion in general. He had also called Cromwell "the vicar of Satan." In 1538, Cromwell convinced the king to arrest Reginald's younger brother and several others of his friends. One of these others was the Marquess of Exeter, whose wife Gertrude had brought the vital information to Chapuys on Mary's behalf.

Mary was terrified at these arrests, but worse was to come. Margaret of Salisbury, now a strong-minded 65-year-old, was also arrested, fiercely questioned, and imprisoned. The only suspicious thing that royal officials found out about the countess was that she possessed a colored design showing Mary's marigolds twined together with pansies, the flower of the Pole family. In Henry's England, you could be arrested for possessing the wrong flower pattern.

Cromwell had now attacked all the Poles within his reach. With his army of spies and informers, he was increasing Henry's power by creating a climate of fear and distrust. No marriage between Mary and Reginald Pole was likely now.

A marriage other than Mary's was in the air at this time, however, namely Henry's own. By now, it was not as easy as it had been to persuade women to marry Henry. Many foreign ladies had their doubts about how safe it might be to become the next queen of England. In fact, Christina of Sweden, a noted beauty, quipped that she wouldn't consider marrying Henry because she had only one head.

By 1539, however, Cromwell had found a willing and acceptable bride for his master. Her name was Anna, and she was the sister of the Duke of

Cleves. Then Anna arrived in England, and disaster struck. No one knows exactly why Henry was so put out with his new fiancée, but he said curtly, "I like her not." It was true that, as the English ladies whispered, her clothing was not fashionable and she spoke hardly any English, and no Latin or French. Nevertheless, Henry went ahead and married Anna on Twelfth Night, January 6, 1540, mainly because he couldn't get out of it. But he immediately began the process of divorcing his new bride. Despite that, Anna asked to remain in England, where she found life much more amusing than in Cleves. Henry, delighted to find a cooperative woman for once, treated her generously, giving her four pleasant country manors and a large income for life. He also saw to it that she ranked high in England, just below the queen (the next one, that is) and the princesses. Thereafter, Anna became quite friendly with Mary. They were about the same age and both unmarried, so they had some things in common.

But Henry took revenge on the man he blamed for the Cleves marriage, and that man was Thomas Cromwell. Like Cardinal Wolsey before him, Cromwell found himself suddenly arrested, condemned, and sent to the Tower. Cromwell the weasel had served Henry the lion for so long that he may have thought he understood this large, selfish, and dangerous king. He was wrong, and on July 28, 1540, he died for it.

On that very same day, Henry married his fifth wife, Kathryn Howard. She was none other than a pretty little niece of Thomas Howard, the Duke of Norfolk (making her first cousin to Ann Boleyn). Princess Mary now had another new stepmother—one who was five years younger than she was. Mary was probably acquainted with the eighteen-year-old Kathryn because she had come to court as one of Anna of Cleves's ladies. There is no surviving portrait of Kathryn, but we know she was petite, sexy, and no stranger to men. It seems Uncle Norfolk had seen in her a perfect way to restore his own fortunes, undermine Cromwell and the religious reformers, and deal a blow to the Seymour brothers, all at once.

Considering his record as a tough-minded military leader and politician, it is amazing that Norfolk took the risk of pushing Kathryn at

Henry. The probability is that Kathryn was the only one of Henry's wives who actually did cheat on him. Kathryn's lover was Thomas Culpeper, a handsome young gentleman of Henry's bedchamber. They began by meeting secretly, but their meetings didn't stay secret for long.

Thomas Howard, Duke of Norfolk, a powerful and devious nobleman who was uncle to both Ann Boleyn and Kathryn Howard.

(A.F. Pollard, *Henry VIII*, 1902)

In the midst of all this royal scheming, Mary had another personal tragedy to bear. In 1541, King Henry decided to execute the Countess of Salisbury for "treason." She had committed no crime except to be a descendant of kings and the mother of the troublesome Cardinal Reginald Pole. This pious and highly respected woman had been a second mother to Mary, advising her, defending her, caring for her when she was sick, and comforting her when she was in despair. Now nearly seventy, a great age for the time, the duchess had at this point been imprisoned in the Tower for over two years. Her death was particularly horrifying because the executioner botched it and had to strike several times. Mary surely spent many hours on her knees praying for the soul of her dear Lady Governess.

Within a few months, more royal blood was shed at the Tower. As was bound to happen eventually, Queen Kathryn got discovered in her infidelity. Henry was stunned when Archbishop Cranmer presented him with the evidence of Kathryn's betrayal. The king still had a romantic streak and had convinced himself that Kathryn truly loved him. He had called her his "blushing rose without a thorn," and now she seemed to be a whole field of thistles. Like Ann, Kathryn was beheaded. Both Mary and nine-year-old Elizabeth saw yet another example of how dangerous it could be to cross their royal father.

The most amazing thing about the fall of Kathryn Howard was that the Duke of Norfolk managed to survive it. He wrote the king a series of oh-so-humble letters in which he blamed Kathryn's behavior on everyone and anyone but himself—his mother-in-law, his sister, his brother and sister-in-law—and declared he was "prostrate at the king's feet."

Mary was now 27 and still unmarried. Her one encounter with a genuine suitor had come a few years earlier when Duke Philip of Bavaria surprised the English court by arriving in person to seek the princess's hand. Philip managed to meet Mary herself in the gardens of the abbey at Enfield. But Mary knew that there could be only one possible answer to Philip: "I will do as my father wishes." Henry toyed with the idea of the match, impressed perhaps with Philip's knight-errant approach to courtship, but though the Bavarian duke continued to seek Mary's hand for a number of years, nothing ever came of it.

King Henry's state of mind after the execution of Kathryn reminds us of the old joke about the man who murdered his parents and then pled for mercy because he was a poor orphan. Certainly Henry felt very lonely and sorry for himself, and the court was quite a gloomy place during the next several months. Henry was now so monstrously fat that it sometimes took six men to carry him about in his chair. The open sores and ulcers on his legs were giving him severe pain. Furthermore, he was 51, in an age when the average life span was 43.

That made him old by anyone's measure. And now the possibility that the king might die set off a contest within the court to see which powerful family would control the little King Edward when Henry was gone. This was the topic of many low-voiced conversations in palace corridors, in taverns, and in country manors during 1542 and the early part of 1543.

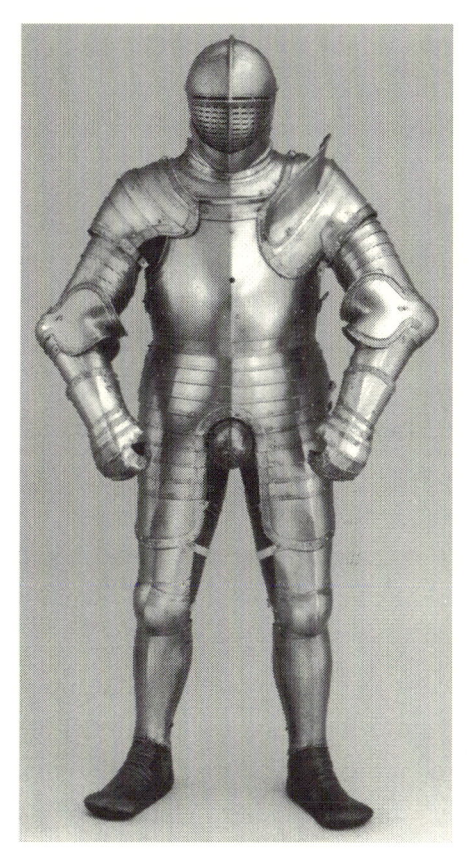

King Henry's love of jousting continued into middle age, even as his girth increased. The suit of armor on the left was made in about 1520 for the king to use in fighting on foot. The suit on the right, designed in about 1540 for tournament and battlefield, fit an older Henry. Both suits of armor were made in Greenwich, England.

(Board of Trustees of the Armouries, Leeds)

But if Henry seemed depressed and old, it had the odd effect of benefiting his daughter Mary. The king now relied on her and sought her company as never before. With no queen at court, it was up to her to act as first lady of the realm. She was now the one who sat with the king at the high table, who led the dancing, who set the fashions. More important, she also had the chance to be there on state occasions, when the king greeted ambassadors, received great nobles, or heard the requests of his more humble subjects. Mary had always kept herself well informed about international affairs because they had affected both her mother's status and her own hopes, first of escape and then of marriage. Now she was able to observe the processes of government at first hand.

Mary learned a great deal from this experience. She certainly had a clear-eyed view of her own prospects for marriage. Chapuys reported her as saying "it was folly to think they would marry her out of England, or even in England, as long as her father lived." That, unfortunately, was the truth.

Yet Mary still had one more stepmother to adjust to. In 1543, her father began paying attention to a 31-year-old widow "of lively and pleasing appearance." Her name was Catherine Parr, Lady Latimer, and in July of that same year she and the king were married.

In choosing Catherine Parr, Henry was at last showing some good sense. Catherine was wise, well educated, sensible, and twice a widow. She was also four years older than Princess Mary, and while not a substitute mother, she was at least someone with considerable experience of life. In addition, Catherine Parr's mother had been one of Mary's mother's favorite ladies. Mary and Elizabeth both attended the small, private wedding, and no one mentioned the fact that Catherine had been very much in love with Jane Seymour's dashing brother Tom before she attracted Henry's attention.

Fortunately for all, Catherine Parr was not Kathryn Howard. There would be no scandal while she took on the task of nursing, amusing, and comforting the old, sick king. In addition, Catherine was probably the closest thing to a mother Elizabeth and Edward would ever know. In fact, she worked at smoothing out the troubled relationships of the whole Tudor family. One result was that both Mary and Elizabeth were restored to their royal status and their places as heirs to the throne, after Edward.

Now, energized by his new marriage, King Henry gave himself one last exciting adventure. In spite of protests from his Council and the Emperor Charles himself, the king led his army to France in a final, glorious war. This was Henry's idea of great fun, and he enjoyed it to the full, although the war itself, like most of his other wars, killed a number of soldiers on both sides and resulted in little concrete gain for the nation. It also cost quite a lot.

By the time Henry returned from the battlefield, he was truly a sick old man. In the last months of 1546, his ulcerated legs gave him a fever that would not yield to treatment. Not that his doctors helped Henry much. In fact, it is probable that an elderly shepherd in a country village would have had better treatment from the local wise woman than most nobles had from their highly trained doctors, who used complicated potions that were useless at best and poisonous at worst. In addition, doctors often cut open the patients' veins to draw blood, thus making them weaker rather than stronger.

It soon became clear that Henry had little time to live. Everyone at court tried to guess who would be regent for the future King Edward, now a round-faced nine-year-old. Should it be Queen Catherine, who was favored by the Lutherans? Or Mary herself, who would have been the choice of the Catholics? In the end, Henry decided from his deathbed that a Council should run the kingdom until Edward was old enough to rule. No doubt Henry hoped that the Council's members would check one another's ambitions and provide a balanced government in which no clique would be able to grab all the power. He was mistaken about that.

Henry died on January 28, 1547, but the Council members kept his death a secret for three days. They even went so far as to order the king's meals served in the great hall as usual, heralded by the sound of trumpets. Meanwhile, Edward Seymour, now Duke of Somerset, established himself as the most powerful man in the new Council. He was, after all, the young king's elder uncle. What more logical than that he should adopt the title of Lord Protector?

Chapter 6

One Young King, Two Old Dukes

At first, it seemed as if Mary could live much as usual under a council headed by Seymour and his supporters. She knew Edward Seymour and his wife Anne Stanhope quite well. She even counted the duchess as a friend, calling her "my good Nan." Furthermore, some of the Council's early actions were reassuring. For example, it repealed most of the treason laws that had made it so fatally easy to convict people like the Countess of Salisbury. But when it came to religion, things were quite different. Both Seymour brothers were now firmly Protestant, as were their major supporters. They soon made it clear that they intended to tilt the balance entirely away from any form of Catholicism and bring in Protestant practices. This last was the sticking point for Mary, and she spent the next six years fighting it.

Meanwhile, the land was ruled by a young boy. Personally, Edward was very fond of his older sister Mary, but he came more and more firmly under the control of the Protector and the Council. There can be no doubt that Edward was a bright boy. He was good at his studies, and he used to write Mary letters in quite elegant Latin. He had his father's fair skin and reddish hair, but he had none of Henry's great size and physical vigor. He also lacked his father's talent for sports, although he did well enough at riding and swordplay. "Imitate your father, the greatest man in the world," said a verse that went with one of Edward's portraits, and Edward did his best by copying Henry's typical wide-legged stance as he posed.

Edward Seymour, the first Lord Protector, Prince Edward's Uncle Ned
(A.F. Pollard, *Henry VIII*, 1902)

The Protector lost no time in arranging his nephew's coronation as King Edward VI. The boy was hailed as "a young king Solomon" as he rode through the streets of London. Along the way there were cheering crowds, and the usual singing and pageants. One of them featured pretty children dressed as Faith, Grace, Nature, Justice, Charity, and Fortune. The boy in the gold-embroidered cloth-of-silver would enjoy the benefits of the first three, but all too little of the last three.

At least, Edward had fun at one part of his coronation. As the procession passed the churchyard of St. Paul's, a Spanish acrobat performed amazing tricks on a rope that had been run from the church steeple to the yard below. The man first slid down the rope on his chest. Edward was delighted, and he signaled his companions to halt so he could watch as the man then reclimbed the rope, using all sorts of fancy footwork and finally hanging by one ankle.

After that came the long coronation ceremony, as redesigned by Archbishop Cranmer. Edward Seymour, Duke of Somerset, was now the most powerful man in the kingdom. He watched with family pride as his brother Tom Seymour took the prizes in all the gala tournaments that followed the ceremony. But on that day, Tom had more on his mind than showing off before the ladies. He had a plan that might make him at least as powerful as his brother.

A royal procession, complete with horsemen, soldiers, hounds, attendants, and even a dragon in the sky. The central figure here is Henry VIII, but the splendor is typically Tudor.

(A. F. Pollard, *Henry VIII*, 1902)

Step one in Tom's plan was to marry into royalty. His sister Jane had been a queen. Why not King Tom? He knew the Council had already begun discussing the "problem" of Princess Mary. She was now heir to the throne, and one of the six wealthiest nobles in the kingdom, under the terms of Henry's will. She was therefore a power on her own estates. She was also beloved by the English people. Why wouldn't she make a suitable bride for Tom Seymour? The two brothers quarreled over the idea, and Tom went on his way, still pursuing his ambitions.

The new Council soon began to bully the princess over religion. A few years before, under extreme pressure, Mary had signed the Oath of Supremacy, recognizing the king as head of the English Church. Now she was ordered to give up something that both her mother and Henry had always taken for granted—the celebration of the mass.

Meanwhile, Mary continued to visit young Edward, but under more and more difficult conditions. It was the Lord Protector's policy to prevent the young king from becoming too fond of anyone but himself and his supporters. The Catholic Mary was definitely not welcome at court. The Council slighted her in a variety of little ways, such as making her sit on a plain bench or cushion when in Edward's presence, and seating her far away from him at table.

In July of 1547, Mary had a visit from Emperor Charles's new ambassador. This was a man named Francis Van der Delft, who had come, after nearly two years, to replace Mary's old and ailing friend and adviser, Eustace Chapuys. Mary invited him to eat with her, the first time she had dined publicly since she went into mourning for her father. They discussed many things—her income (too small, according to the ambassador), her dowry (since Mary still hoped to be allowed to marry), and the most intriguing piece of recent court gossip. Tom Seymour, the Lord High Admiral, was still working toward his own advancement. Since he had failed to wed a future queen (Mary herself), he had secretly married a former queen, his old love Catherine Parr. Sadly, Catherine died in childbirth only a little more than a year later.

Mary had had little contact with her friend Catherine after she married Tom Seymour, which was probably just as well. Instead, Mary lived quietly on her chief estates, which were (not accidentally) just far enough from London to keep her away from the court, but close enough so the Council could keep an eye on her. Soon, however, events over which Mary had no control brought her into the national spotlight.

In the spring and summer of 1549, a series of rebellions and protests broke out in various parts of England. The people had good reason for discontent. Policies of both the late King Henry and the Lord Protector had caused prices to rise and money to drop in value. Ordinary people couldn't pay the rent to their landlords or buy the foodstuffs they needed. Many were hungry and homeless. Once, poor people had received charity from the monasteries, but the monasteries were gone. Bands of rebels sprang up in at least six counties, demanding economic reforms and restoration of the mass and the monasteries.

The largest rebellion, led by a leather tanner named Robert Kett, included between 10,000 and 20,000 men. This gave the Council members a severe fright. King Henry had faced a few uprisings of this kind, and he had put them down by prompt action and sheer force of personality. But the old king was gone, and the Councilors knew they were on their own.

They sent John Dudley, Duke of Northumberland, to put down Kett's uprising. Dudley was a very able military man. He succeeded in defeating the rebels, and his paid German troops slaughtered more than 3,000 men. The rebel leaders, including Kett, were captured and hanged.

Even though they had won, the Council members had learned a disturbing lesson. There were many discontented people in the country, and they might rise up again in support of a popular leader—someone like an attractive and very Catholic princess. But the Council thought it had a powerful weapon with which to bring Mary to heel and assure that the Catholics would never rally around her. Already that year, the Councilors had passed the Act of Uniformity, a law that made it a crime to hold any religious services other than those of the Reformed (Protestant) Church. Then they sent the Council's secretary and the current chancellor, the well-named Sir Richard Rich, to tell Mary that she and all her household were forbidden to hear mass, even privately.

These were grown men, yet it seemed they had their heads buried in the muddy tidal flats of the Thames River. After all, the royal court was a small, closed circle, and Princess Mary had known most of these people all her life. There were in fact only 56 peers (nobles with the title of duke, marquess, earl, viscount, or baron) in the whole realm of England at this time. Mary would have remembered, no doubt, that it was Richard Rich's false testimony that had helped execute Sir Thomas More, whom many saw as a martyr to the Catholic faith. Rich and the others sent by the Council had done terrible things, in her eyes. They had not only made themselves rich on monastery lands, they had actually drunk from cups once used for holy communion and eaten from plates that once held communion wafers. She had every reason to despise these men.

Moreover, for nearly twenty years, Mary had been saying no to powerful men who tried to force her to betray her mother and her religion. She had no trouble telling Rich and his allies no again. After they left, she instructed her chaplains to say more, rather than fewer masses each day. She even invited her Catholic neighbors to join her, since there were no more Catholic services in the local churches. Her reputation as a courageous leader increased day by day.

Mary had won this time, but she knew perfectly well that she could not win forever. The political situation grew trickier as the leadership of the Council split apart. The trouble had started with the fall of Tom Seymour earlier that same year. Uncle Tom actually invaded the young Edward's bedchamber, apparently intending to kidnap him and claim the protectorship for himself. It was a terrifying moment for twelve-year-old Edward, who saw his favorite uncle kill one of his pet dogs when it tried to protect its young master. Not surprisingly, the plan failed. Seymour was captured by the king's guards, charged with high treason, and executed.

Protector Edward Seymour managed to survive this crisis, barely. (With remarkable lack of family feeling, Seymour even signed his own brother's death warrant.) However, the summer rebellions of that same year had seriously frayed the last strands of his authority. And who did the final cutting of those strands but John Dudley, Duke of Northumberland, the military hero who in some people's eyes had saved the country from Kett's pro-Catholic rebels? Northumberland had Seymour arrested and briefly imprisoned. After that, Northumberland was soon the new Protector and firmly in charge of the Council.

This was a bad change for Mary. Whereas Edward Seymour had merely wanted to keep her in the background, Northumberland was a much more intelligent and dangerous man. He liked to pull strings from behind the scenes and had a personal scheme at least as ambitious as the former Lord High Admiral's. It was a scheme for controlling the throne in which Mary played no part at all. Northumberland saw very clearly that Mary had assumed leadership of the country's Catholics. Well-bred Catholic girls competed with each other for positions in her household as if it had been a top boarding school (which in terms of the time it was). Wherever she went, especially at her estates in Norfolk, she was greeted by devout followers of the Old Religion who were anxious to tell her their grievances and hear her priests say mass. To these people, she appeared as a tower of strength. Few of them knew of the fears she confided to Ambassador Van der Delft or the pleas for support she sent to the Emperor.

The Council under Northumberland saw her as the means "by which the rats of Rome might creep into their stronghold." They were not the only ones to use colorful language. Mary herself told Van der Delft that English Catholics were in a situation like that of the ancient Israelites held captive in Egypt by the wicked pharaoh. She predicted that God would send down upon England plagues more horrid than those that had forced the release of Moses and his people. For a time, it seemed as if she was right. More than 50,000 people died of the sweating sickness in 1550.

Ambassador Van der Delft hoped that Dudley's rise to power might benefit Mary's cause. After all, Dudley had ousted the strongly Protestant

Seymour. But Mary quickly set the ambassador straight. She had always paid close attention to the politics of the court, even when she could not take part. The duke, she told Van der Delft, was "the most unstable man in England" and his overthrow of Edward Seymour had nothing to do with any religious disagreement and everything to do with his own ambitions. Unfortunately, she was right about that, too.

Perhaps, however, there was a better way out. By 1550, Mary was deeply involved in another plot to escape from England. It happened that Ambassador Van der Delft was not in good health and intended to return home. He thought he could smuggle Mary away with him. His replacement, Jehan Scheyfve, was not to know of the escape. That way, he could deny it if he came to be questioned.

On Sunday, June 29, the Flemish ships came in sight of the English coast, close to Mary's manor of Woodham Walter. The plan was for her to ride secretly to the coast, board a small boat used to carry grain, and be ferried out to the fleet. But the plot began to go wrong almost at once. First, the boatman decided he couldn't risk it. Then Mary's supporters reported that the whole coast was suddenly alive with watchers and spies, ready to report any unusual activity. Obviously, this particular night was not the right one. Van der Delft sailed away without Mary, and though he had promised to return for her, he could not. He died in Flanders, muttering about the English princess and how it was his duty to save her.

Now Mary had no one but Van der Delft's secretary, Jehan Dubois. Together they made a new plan, much like the old one. On July 1, the Flemish rescue ships duly appeared. But at this point, something upset Mary so badly that she sent a message to say she was not coming after all. Dubois wanted to escape at once, but he was persuaded to go to a local graveyard for a meeting with Sir Robert Rochester, Mary's household controller. Long past midnight, the two men talked in the dark. Sir Robert reported that it was not safe for Mary to leave. There were spies in her household. Besides, Rochester whispered, King Edward was very ill and perhaps dying. All things considered, he declared, it was a poor idea for the heir to the throne to flee the country. The fact that Rochester's information was based on a horoscope, not on a medical report, comes as no surprise in an age when nearly everyone believed in astrology, prophecies, signs, and portents.

Mary herself was torn by doubt at this moment. Dubois was there; the tide was favorable; perhaps she ought to go. At the same time, she had been warned that the town officials had doubled the watch and were on the lookout for her. For one of the few times in her life, Mary gave way to her fears, crying out over and over, "What will become of me?" Maybe she would be ready to go on Friday, she said, maybe not at all.

Though some historians have charged that Mary acted "just like a woman" at this point, being unable to make up her mind, it is hard to know what decision she could or should have made. If she tried to leave, she might well be arrested and imprisoned. If Edward died while she was in a foreign land, she would never be queen. And if she stayed, she might be arrested anyway, considering that word of her plans seemed to have leaked out already. In the end, she urged Dubois to leave without her and wait for a more favorable time. But that time never came. Perhaps a spy told the Council of her intentions. Perhaps Northumberland was simply shrewd enough to foresee what Mary might try to do. Either way, the Council made certain that Mary had no more chances to leave England. Instead, they planned to force her to obey the Act of Uniformity, stop hearing mass, and thus lose her place as leader of the Catholic cause.

In March of 1551, Mary decided to go to London and speak for herself. She had no intention of looking as if she were begging favors from the Council, however. When she set out for the capital, it was with a great following. Fifty knights and gentlemen clothed in velvet rode before her; eighty gentlemen and ladies rode behind her, and each one wore a set of Catholic rosary beads, which underlined the nature of their mission. As word of Mary's coming reached the city, crowds poured out to welcome her. By the time she arrived, more than 400 people had joined the procession. Some members of the crowd claimed afterward that they had seen visions of armed men in the clouds as she approached, that there had been three suns in the sky, and that the earth shook beneath her feet. So many people came out into the narrow streets to greet her that the velvet-clad knights had a hard time pushing through the throng.

This display was most unwelcome to Northumberland and the Council, who made a point of snubbing the princess by not giving her an official welcome. Instead, they had her brought straight before Edward and the entire Council. All in all, Mary handily won the debate that followed. She ended by making a personal appeal to Edward, reminding him that her soul existed to serve God and her body to serve His Majesty. She also said she would rather die than give up the Old Religion.

Edward, of course, had been hearing nothing but ill of Mary for some time—how stubborn she was, and how disloyal. Now he was moved, at least enough to assure her he had no desire to take her life. No one knows, however, whether Mary might not have been arrested the next day if the Emperor Charles had not sent a formal message saying he would declare war if the princess was not allowed to practice her religion.

Mary had never believed she could win over the Council by argument, and she had known full well the risk she took by riding to London at all. She had come because of her conscience and her honor.

Partly as a result of the emperor's threat, Northumberland did nothing further about the inconvenient princess. In fact, three of the king's most powerful bishops were now advising that although it would be wrong to give Mary actual permission to hear mass, it would be honorable (in their terms) to look the other way, at least for a while. It is a great shame that neither side stuck to the bishops' calm and sensible plan.

The Council allowed Mary to leave for her manor of Beaulieu a few days later. She might have gone sooner, but she had been sick, possibly from the strain of the interview. Mary was one of those people who can be strong and decisive in public but suffer for it later in private.

The Council's next move shows how little they understood Mary, and also something about the general attitude to women at that time. The Council summoned her household controller, Sir Robert Rochester, and two other officials to appear before them in London. On one level, of course, the Councilors did this to frighten Mary. But they also seemed to believe that if the princess were told by her own (male) servants that hearing mass was a bad idea, she would give in and be a good girl. That they were wrong was made perfectly clear by the three men, who stated definitely that Mary was mistress in her own house, and they were her servants. She never asked their advice on matters of religion, they said, nor would they presume to offer it. For this piece of frankness, they were all three arrested and taken to the Tower.

The Council then sent Richard Rich (who had recently been named lord chancellor) and two others to Mary a second time, at one of her residences called Copt Hall. This time, their mission was to tell her the game was up. They were armed with a letter from the young king, ordering her to stop hearing mass immediately. Mary would have none of this. First of all, she reminded them that they owed their present positions to her father King Henry, who had raised them up from humble origins. Who were they to give orders to her, a princess? Then, changing her tone, Mary went down on her knees, saying that she was loyal to King Edward in all things except those that were between herself and God. The three Councilors should not have been surprised to hear this, since Mary (and Katharine before her) had been making this same speech in public since 1527.

Mary could not, however, prevent the Council's men from calling her household together, including her three chaplains, and forbidding them directly from saying or hearing any religious service except the new Protestant one. If they did, they were warned, they would be arrested for treason. This was a serious blow, but not quite as serious as the Council hoped. For Mary had *four* chaplains, not three, and one of them had succeeded in hiding himself away during the confrontation. So, although

Mary sent the other chaplains away for their own protection, there was still one who could rightly claim he had never been ordered to stop saying mass for Mary. The three envoys knew about the missing chaplain, and while their men tried once again to find him, Mary managed to get in the last word. Opening a window, she leaned out and called to them that she hoped they would soon send back her controller, the faithful Robert Rochester. Since his arrest, she explained wryly, "I take the accounts myself, and lo! I have learned how many loaves of bread be made of a bushel of wheat! I know my mother and father never brought me up to brewing and baking and, to be plain with you, I am weary of my office." The little page boys, the ladies in waiting, all the household servants heard her. Some part of their loyalty may have been due to the fact that Mary could joke even while under attack.

Nevertheless, the Council had won a major point. Mary was forced to give up her practice of inviting outsiders into her house for religious services. Luckily for her, the Council was soon taken up with a new scandal. In October 1551, Edward Seymour the former Lord Protector was arrested again. Seymour was convicted, and his execution took place early in 1552. Jane Seymour had escaped from this world by dying of natural causes; now both her brothers had died on the block.

In the midst of this uproar, Mary's three officers were released and allowed to return to her household. No one paid much attention. The Council was tearing itself apart, one clique against another. In fact, a few weeks before the arrest of Seymour, Northumberland had asked for Mary's help. He even hinted that he would make her regent and restore the Old Religion. Fortunately, Mary was too smart and too wary to believe him. If she had put herself in his power, it might have proved a fatal mistake.

In the aftermath of Edward Seymour's death, the Duke of Northumberland took steps he thought would assure his own future. One of his chief supporters was Henry Grey, Marquess of Dorset. Grey's wife was none other than Frances Brandon, the daughter of Charles

Brandon and Princess Mary the Tudor Rose. Frances was thus the niece of Henry VIII, with a large dollop of royal blood in her veins. Dorset and Northumberland now announced the forthcoming marriage of Northumberland's drunken and thoroughly unpleasant second son, Guildford Dudley, to the oldest of Dorset's three daughters, Lady Jane Grey. This wedding was to take place in the spring of 1553. By that time, it seemed likely that King Henry's beloved son Edward VI had not long to live.

Chapter 7

The Miraculous Year

Of all the children of Henry VIII, the one with the saddest life story is Edward. Motherless from birth, he had been a fair, round-faced baby whose good looks and sturdy health were much praised by the court ladies. Yet this child grew up into a bright but frustrated and sickly teenager, already ill with the tuberculosis that had killed his father's brother Arthur and his bastard half-brother Henry Fitzroy. Few people seem to have cared about Edward's happiness and well-being. The only exceptions were his sisters Mary and Elizabeth (who were mostly kept away from him) and some of his lower-ranking servants (who were powerless to help him).

After the death of his father when he was eleven, Edward's every move, and practically his every thought, were controlled by his two Lords Protector, "Uncle Ned" Seymour and the Duke of Northumberland. It would have taken a saint or a wimp to put up with this situation, and Edward was neither. The depth of his wretchedness showed in a distressing confrontation he had with some of his household officers and "governors," who were more like velvet-clad jailers. One day, the young king seized a pet falcon from her perch, plucked out her feathers and then tore the poor bird to pieces, crying out in anguish that his advisers were plucking him in the same way but that someday he would have his revenge and tear *them* to pieces. This cry for help went unanswered, and soon (as Edward's tuberculosis worsened) it was too late.

By early summer 1553, the Council knew their young ruler was dying. Protector Northumberland's chief concerns were to keep Catholic Mary from the throne and to ensure that he and his friends continued to control a young, powerless ruler. First, however, the Protector had to make a visit to King Edward's bedside. From the feverish boy who was coughing blood, the duke managed to get a signed document changing the list of heirs to the throne. Mary and Elizabeth were both out. Instead, the crown would go—guess where? To the heirs of King Henry's great-niece Lady Jane Grey (granddaughter of Mary the Tudor Rose). And Jane was about to be married (quite unwillingly) to Northumberland's son Guildford Dudley. What a coincidence!

Meanwhile, Mary had reason to suspect what was coming. Her sorrow over Edward, the little boy who had loved her and sent her gifts and Latin letters, was mixed with both fear and determination. She had said she did not expect the Protector to let her live if anything happened to Edward. At the same time, she knew that she, and only she, was the lawful heir to the throne according to the will of her father.

Northumberland needed time. He needed time to gather his supporters and complete his plans, to send soldiers to important castles, to collect weapons and money and supplies in case there was a rebellion in Mary's favor. Pathetically, Edward was all but ignored as he lay dying, dosed with opium and poisonous "medicine" made with arsenic. At last, on July 6, 1553, Edward's suffering ended.

Shortly before the young king's death, Northumberland sent messages to both Mary and Elizabeth, summoning them to their brother's bedside at Greenwich. Neither one was foolish enough to come. Elizabeth, who at twenty had one of the shrewdest brains in the kingdom, assessed the situation, decided it was not her time, and did nothing.

Princess Elizabeth about the age of fourteen. This portrait was painted around 1547, the year of King Henry's death.
(A. F. Pollard, *Henry VIII*, 1902)

Mary moved. With only two of her women and six guards, she rode at night from her manor of Hunsdon toward Kenninghall, which was nearer to London. In this way she gave the impression of obeying Northumberland's summons. But obedience was not on her mind. She was at Euston Hall on July 8, when she received an urgent message. Her personal goldsmith, a man named Robert Raynes, had ridden from London with all speed to tell her that Edward was dead. By the next day, she was at Kenninghall and the news was confirmed. Only then did she summon her household—everyone from the great Catholic lords to the lowliest laundress, stable hand, and pot boy from the kitchens. She told them that "by divine and human law" she was now queen of England. The hall rang with cheers.

Mary had planned ahead for this moment, as events quickly showed. Immediately, she sent messages to the country round and a stream of gentlemen began to flock toward Kenninghall. These were not the great nobles, they were knights and local landowners. But they came with men and money and weapons and wagonloads of foodstuffs, none of which could have been gathered together overnight. Obviously, they were all on the alert and ready for the summons. More than thirty individuals and their followers arrived in the next three days.

Meanwhile, in London, the Protector had made his move. On July 9 he proclaimed, in the name of the late, lamented King Edward, that the nation's new ruler was Lady Jane Grey (now Dudley), aged sixteen. Protector Northumberland had given the crown to a sweet, scholarly, unprepared, very Protestant queen who would naturally do exactly what she was told by her father-in-law Northumberland and her father, the Marquess of Dorset. At the same time, Northumberland took control of the Tower of London, locked the Council inside it, and brought "Queen Jane" to the Tower's royal apartments.

On the surface, Northumberland held all the cards. He controlled London and made sure everyone knew it. (A young man named Gilbert Pot, for example, was sent to the pillory and had his ears cut off, merely for "speaking certain words of Queen Mary.") Northumberland also controlled the Tower's huge stores of arms and supplies. He controlled the Council. And he was the best all-round army commander in England. The only thing he needed to do was send someone to arrest Mary. If Northumberland had succeeded, he would have been the effective ruler of the country.

What happened next surprised no one more than Northumberland. First of all, Mary moved her forces to Framlingham Castle, which was protected by thirteen great towers plus walls forty feet high and eight feet thick. There, she was more or less safe from arrest. Then she sent a letter to the Council, announcing that she was claiming the throne. Reports from other areas also began to arrive in London. Lord Thus-and-So was marching to join Mary from Sussex. Sir Thomas Such-and-such was leading his Norfolk men to her side. And everywhere there were "innumerable companies of the common people" who dropped what they were doing and went to the support of their princess, the daughter of "Old King Hal."

The Protector had not planned on leaving London, but now it was obvious that someone would have to confront Mary's forces. Northumberland and his army marched north and made it as far as Cambridge. Meanwhile, in Yarmouth Harbor, about thirty miles from Framlingham, there were seven great ships of war. A captain loyal to Mary had himself rowed out to the fleet and urged the sailors to declare for her as queen. Inspired by his words, the 2,000 sailors rebelled against their officers. By the next day, they had joined Mary's forces, bringing with them 100 large cannons from the ships. This was not good news for Northumberland.

Word of the events at Yarmouth reached London, where the Council members in the Tower began to rethink their positions. Maybe Mary *wasn't* going to be the loser. A dozen of them managed to force their way past the guards, left the Tower, and offered a reward for the arrest of Northumberland. One leader of this group was the Earl of Arundel, who was to play an important role during Mary's reign.

The next day, the escaped Council members appeared together in the center of London and proclaimed Mary Queen of England. The city went wild with joy. Most ordinary people had always taken the common-sense view that King Henry's children should succeed him, regardless of past history, religion, or politics. They knew Mary for her kindness, dignity, and courage in the face of bullying by the authorities. In contrast, Northumberland, like Protector Seymour, had made a lot of enemies through his greed, double dealing, and overbearing manner. Now church bells began to ring for Mary, and people literally danced in the streets. They threw their hats in the air, and the rich tossed purses full of coins to the crowd. Someone who was there reported that the noise was so great, what with the bells and the cheering, that speech was nearly impossible.

Jane Grey's father, the Marquess of Dorset, took a good look at this scene and caved in. Northumberland, too, realized the jig was up. Without a second thought, these fathers abandoned Jane and Guildford, the two frightened teenagers whom they had tried to set on the throne, and set about saving their own necks. By the next day, Mary's camp was receiving a constant stream of great lords coming to beg her pardon for supporting Jane Grey. Mary had won without firing a shot.

By August 3, both Northumberland and Dorset were in custody. Mary entered London with a guard of several thousand, her gown made of purple velvet with a kirtle and underskirt of purple satin decorated with gold work and pearls. She was followed by Princess Elizabeth, with a thousand gentlemen of her own, and Gertrude, Marchioness of Exeter.

Mary was met by London's Lord Mayor and Recorder, who presented her with a royal scepter. Mary thanked them "with so smiling a countenance that the hearers wept for joy." She then rode on toward the Tower, where London's main store of arms was kept. There, she found a reminder that she might have come to the Tower under much grimmer circumstances. By the Tower's gate, she found the Duke of Norfolk, Bishop Gardiner, and Edward Earl of Courtenay (the son of Gertrude of Exeter and her executed husband, Lord Montague). All of them knelt and asked her to pardon them for the crimes that had sent them to the Tower, and Mary did pardon them, probably with great pleasure in the cases of the Catholic Bishop Gardiner and her friend's son Courtenay. That she also pardoned the Duke of Norfolk, who had caused such pain and sorrow to Katharine and herself, can only be seen as a sign of Mary's forgiving nature.

Even before she was crowned queen, Mary had to form her government. She would certainly need a Council, whose members would carry out her policies and oversee various aspects of administration. Mary kept some holdovers from the previous Council because she knew she needed their experience. Also, she couldn't afford to offend England's Protestants by shutting them out of the government. Perhaps to balance these officers, Mary appointed the old Duke of Norfolk to the office of Earl Marshal and had him preside over the treason trial of John Dudley, Duke of Northumberland. The duke was found guilty and executed, but Mary showed herself unexpectedly merciful in releasing Jane Grey's father, the Marquess of Dorset. Jane herself and her husband Guildford Dudley still remained in the Tower, separated but in comfortable quarters. Mary was well aware that Jane was only sixteen and had never even thought of being queen until days before her hasty and rather depressing coronation. In Biblical terms, Mary was not inclined to visit the sins of the fathers upon the children.

Another thing Mary said she had no intention of doing was to force anyone to follow her own Catholic faith. She made that quite clear to the emperor's new ambassador, Simon Renard. Of course, she saw to it that the people could again hear the Latin mass, make religious pilgrimages, and so on. But she did not punish anyone for following the Protestant form of service in Archbishop Cranmer's *Book of Common Prayer.*

Since its construction was begun nearly a thousand years ago, the Tower of London has been a fortress, a royal residence, a prison, an armory, and home to the royal zoo. This view shows the Tower about 1906.
(*Pictorial London,* 1906)

By the end of September 1553, everything was ready for Mary's coronation. For weeks, there had been frantic preparation. Painters and carpenters created triumphal arches, wagons, barges, and platforms for performers. Seamstresses sewed costumes, artists painted masks, choirs and musicians practiced hymns of praise, and poets hastily composed flattering verses in Latin and English. Courtiers sent for their best jewels, bishops got out their finest vestments, colorful banners and hangings were sewn, and an acrobat practiced his routine. (This one was Dutch, not Spanish, as at Edward's coronation.)

In accordance with tradition, Mary moved into the royal apartments in the Tower. There, she learned all the complicated rituals and speeches and responses necessary for her coronation. She also introduced a new element into the event, which was all her own. She called together the members of her Council, went on her knees before them, and began to speak with great emotion about the duties and responsibilities of ruling, about her devotion to the country, and about the solemn tasks in which she would need their help. Never before had a sovereign made such a humble and heartfelt appeal. The Councilors were so moved by "the queen's great goodness and integrity" that many were in tears.

Finally, on the day before the coronation, the people had the satisfaction of seeing the queen herself. Mary rode in a litter covered in white cloth-of-gold, which was pulled by six horses in white trappings. Her costume was also made from white cloth-of-gold, trimmed with the rich white fur called miniver. Her red-gold hair was held by a glittering jeweled net, and she was crowned with "a round circlet of gold, much like a hooped garland," which contained many spectacular jewels. The circlet was so heavy she sometimes had to rest her head in her hand. Above her was a royal canopy carried by a company of knights.

The procession made many stops to see pageants in Mary's honor. One compared her to the biblical heroine Judith, who freed her people by cutting off the head of Holofernes (meaning the Duke of Northumberland). She was also compared to Athena, the Greek goddess of wisdom. But perhaps the most appropriate comparison would have been with the Dutch acrobat who balanced so dangerously atop the church's weather vane. Mary was 37, an age by which most women were married with several children. Instead, she had spent the last sixteen years walking a tightrope stretched over a long drop into political and personal disaster.

On October 1, 1553, Mary went to her coronation in Westminster Cathedral. The ceremony was performed by Stephen Gardiner, who was now both Lord Chancellor and Bishop of Winchester. Gardiner was assisted by ten other bishops and all Mary's private chaplains. Dressed in the crimson robes she would wear when she addressed Parliament, Mary was led to the great gilded throne whose last occupant had been so much smaller and younger. She was presented to the people at each of the high platform's four corners. Then she received the symbols of a ruling sovereign—the orb, a golden globe that stood for the world; the sword, with which she must protect her people; and two scepters because she was both king and queen. The entire ceremony lasted from ten in the morning through mid-afternoon. Finally, touched with holy oil, crowned, and blessed by holy hands, Mary received the oaths of her nobles. Each one placed his hands between hers and recited the ancient pledge of support, "to live and to die, against all manner of folk, so help me God and all hallows." Some of these oaths were kept. Others were not worth much more than the crumbs from the upcoming banquet.

The importance of food and feasting in Tudor society is hard to understand unless one remembers that a bad harvest or a war could still cause widespread starvation at this time. Food therefore became a statement of wealth and well-being, almost as much as cloth-of-gold or crimson velvet. At Mary's coronation banquet, held in the Great Hall at Westminster, the queen was served with an astonishing number of dishes—312, to be exact. These dishes were brought to the table in groups called courses, and each course was heralded by a musical fanfare.

From a modern point of view, the foods of the Tudor court probably looked better than they tasted. In the first place, a great deal of the food was stale or nearly rotten by the time it reached the table. For that reason, cooks did all they could to cover up the taste with strong (and expensive) spices such as cloves, pepper, ginger, and cinnamon, as well as flavors we would consider perfumes, such as rosewater, sweetbriar, violet, and musk. Fruits were also used to flavor meat, and additional sweetening came from cane sugar, which at this time was a luxury for the rich, as was rice. Many dishes had unfamiliar names such as frumenty (flavored grain boiled in milk), bucknade (meat chopped with nuts, dried fruit, onions, and spices), pumpes (meatballs), or mortrews (meat ground in a mortar with hot spices and egg yolk, then boiled in a cloth bag). Noticeably missing from the menus of the rich were vegetables, dairy products (called "white meat"), and salads, which were considered country-people's food. This meant that the poor may actually have had healthier diets than their "betters" as they got more vitamin C and calcium.

Everyone drank ale, beer, or wine (for the rich) with meals, as the water supply was unhealthy. One of the typical housewife's duties was to brew ale for her family. Naturally, Mary did not make her own ale, but this was the kind of brewing she had taunted the Council's envoys about, a few years before at Copt Hall.

Since Mary was always described as thin, she probably didn't take more than a taste of most of the 312 dishes at the coronation banquet. Her father would have gratified the cooks by eating a great deal more. Huge quantities of food—4,900 dishes—were left over and given out to the people at the palace gates, in accordance with tradition.

Inside the hall, another ancient tradition was being fulfilled. Throughout the meal, the Earl Marshal and the High Steward of England kept order—on horseback. Then a third horseman rode into the hall in full armor. He was Sir Edward Dymoke, the royal champion. He threw down a mailed gauntlet to show he was issuing a challenge, and a herald called it out so everyone could hear: "If there be any manner of man, of what estate, degree, or condition soever he be, that will say and maintain that our Sovereign Lady, Queen Mary the First, this day here present, is not the rightful and undoubted inheritrix [heir] to the imperial crown of this realm of England, and that of right she ought not to be crowned Queen, I say he lieth like a false traitor, and that I am ready the same to maintain with him whilst I have breath in my body!"

The challenge was repeated in all four corners of the hall, and when no one took up the gauntlet and offered to fight, Dymoke turned his horse to face the queen. Mary lifted her cup, drank to her champion, and then gave him the cup as a reward for a duty well done.

Mary's waiting was over. She was now the crowned and rightful queen of a green and pleasant realm containing about 70,000 square miles, close to the size of Oklahoma. In the 1530s, one of her father's officials had traveled over its length and breadth, missing "neither cape nor bay, haven, creek or pier, river nor confluence of rivers, beaches, washes, lakes, meres, fenny [meaning swampy] waters, mountains, valleys, moors, heaths, forests, woods, cities, boroughs, castles, principal manor places, monasteries and colleges." All these features were still to be found in Mary's England, except of course the monasteries. There were about 3,500,000 women, men, and children in the land. By far the largest city was the nation's capital, London, with a population of about 80,000, comparable to that of many very small cities in the United States today. Far behind London were the cities of Norwich and Bristol, each with a little over 10,000 inhabitants—hardly large enough to be called cities in modern terms.

The people of this realm lived largely by farming, as their ancestors had done for thousands of years. They raised mostly wheat, rye, and barley, which were ground into flour or meal by windmills or water mills. Next after farming came fishing. English fishermen sailed as far west as Iceland and the banks of Newfoundland to bring back cod and halibut, or as far east as the Baltic Sea in their quest for herring. The land was also rich in coal, tin, lead, copper, and iron, but mining was dangerous and not very efficient.

Yet even in Mary's lifetime, the land had changed significantly. Landowners were turning more and more crop lands into sheep pasture, enclosing the fields with fences. Now one shepherd might work where several farm families had once rented land and made a living. But sheep were more profitable than grain, because wool fed Europe's vast demand for woven cloth. The so-called "enclosures," coupled with the closing of the monasteries, had left many people unemployed, so that there were complaints about beggars, robbers, and even "hookers," who were given to stealing people's clothes off clothes lines by reaching over fences with long, hooked poles.

In his 38-year reign, King Henry had raised England's standing in the eyes of Europe, but the quarreling, scheming, and dishonesty of Edward's

Council had dropped it to almost nothing in a short six years. The English of 1553 were not desperate, but they were not very happy, either.

These were now Mary's people. They owed her reverence, because rulers were chosen by God's will. They owed her loyalty and obedience, to fight her wars and defeat her enemies. And they owed her taxes, which had to be voted by Parliament. She owed them care and protection—from foreign invaders, from robbers and criminals, from injustice in the courts, and from other dangers such as witchcraft and heresy. This was the time-honored bond between a people and its ruler. Mary now had to decide how she was going to fulfill her part of the bargain.

Chapter 8

"What I Am, Ye Right Well Know"

*I*n a very real sense, Mary Tudor considered that she had married the realm of England at her coronation. Indeed, in years to come, she would refer to the nation as her first husband. Yet if there was one thing on which Mary and her subjects were agreed, it was that she needed to marry an honest-to-goodness husband, and soon.

If Mary had daydreamed about love, she would hardly have taken her father's married life for a model. But her own Aunt Mary, the Tudor Rose, had one of the most romantic, and by all accounts the happiest, marriages of the age, a story Mary the Queen certainly knew well.

King Henry's younger sister Mary was said by many to be the loveliest woman of her time, admired for her dark hair and white skin as if she had been Snow White. Mary loved the king's good friend Charles Brandon, but King Henry informed her that she was to wed the aging, widowed King of France, Louis XII. Mary knew her duty, and she knew Henry wouldn't take no for an answer, but she made a typically Tudor bargain with the all-powerful king, her brother. If Louis died (*when* Louis died), she would be free to pick her next husband herself.

In the fall of 1514, Mary was shipped off to France with a lot of gowns and gold plate and jewels. Four months later, Louis was dead. Lovely Mary was a childless widow, and Charles, newly created Duke of Suffolk,

Princess Mary, "The Tudor Rose," and Charles Brandon, Duke of Suffolk, the husband for whom she braved the anger of her brother, King Henry.

(A. F. Pollard, *Henry VIII*, 1902)

was one of the nobles sent to bring her home to England. Instead, Mary sweet-talked the new French king, Francis I, into letting her marry Charles right there in France. Both Mary and Charles knew that Henry would be furious (he was already planning Mary's next foreign marriage), but they took the risk, hoping that the king was too fond of both of them to stay mad for long. They were more or less right. Henry sulked and didn't let them come home for three months, but how bad could a French honeymoon be? Then Henry told them he had forgiven them. Back in England, Mary and Charles Brandon seem to have been extremely happy, and their niece Mary would have grown up knowing the love story of this strong-minded princess. Could it be her turn now?

Even before Mary was crowned queen, many people, including most of the Council, assumed that there was only one possible man for her to marry. Edward Courtenay, the son of Mary's dear and loyal friend Marchioness Gertrude of Exeter, was one of the three great nobles she had freed in August when she arrived to take over the Tower of London. Courtenay was a rather good-looking young Catholic with a decent education in literature, science, the classics, and music. These characteristics, many people thought, might form a bond between him and Mary.

Unfortunately, however, observers noted other traits in Courtenay. He was arrogant, poor, stubborn, and inexperienced in life and in government. He was also reckless, quarrelsome, and vengeful. In short order, Mary concluded that Courtenay was absolutely impossible as a suitor, despite the hopes of Bishop Gardiner and many others. She gave him the title to his grandfather's earldom of Devonshire, presented him with an enormous diamond, and encouraged him to leave the country.

Meanwhile, certain parts of England were seething like a pot of venison broth. The Catholics had been unhappy during Edward's reign; now the Protestants were alarmed at the prospect of Queen Mary's. Preachers gave fiery sermons predicting ruin for the nation under a Catholic queen.

Naturally, when it came to Mary's marriage, the English Protestants would have preferred a Protestant prince. But Mary's thoughts were turning to the Emperor Charles V, who was, in her eyes, the one remaining man of her family and the one who had stood by her during all the frightening and difficult years gone by. Mary didn't know, because none of his ambassadors had ever told her, of the many times when Charles had failed to act on her behalf and made it clear that he had little personal concern for her.

Charles was in his mid-fifties now, weighed down by the cares of state. He longed to hand over his vast empire to be shared between his younger brother Ferdinand and his son Philip. The possibility of a marriage with Prince Philip had been suggested to Mary by Ambassador Renard even before young Edward's death, and she was well acquainted with his reputation.

The 26-year-old Philip had been married before, but his wife had recently died. He was widely said to be handsome, dignified, and pious. Yet not everything Mary heard about Philip was favorable. For example, he was far from popular within his father's empire. It was also rumored that in terms of illicit affairs, he would have made *Henry VIII* look like a monk. This last worried Mary a great deal, and she begged Renard to reassure her that Philip was of good character. Of course, the ambassador did reassure her. It was what he was paid for. (Renard's name in French means "the fox" and it was quite appropriate.) He even told Mary an outright lie, saying that Philip himself was eager for the marriage. The truth was that Philip felt he owed obedience to his father, but he often referred to Mary, then and later, as his aunt. This is not a word used by an eager bridegroom. (She was in fact his first cousin once removed.)

By the time her coronation was over, Mary and her Council were seriously discussing the match with Philip. There was at least one major problem, however. The English people did not like Spain (which Philip was scheduled to inherit) and were horrified at the idea that if Mary married a foreigner, he would naturally become their king and have control of their lives. Mary was aware of these fears and had no intention of giving up her right to rule England. But neither her people nor Philip knew that.

By the end of October 1553, Mary had made up her mind. She announced that Prince Philip was her final choice, her perfect love. She added that once she had made a decision, she would never change it. This was a promise Mary could be relied on to keep. It was her nature to be steadfast, even stubborn.

Meanwhile, Mary had a kingdom to rule. Into this job, she threw herself with a determination that astonished the men around her. She would rise at dawn, hear mass, and start work right afterward, not even taking time to eat until well after noon, and continuing to handle state business by candlelight until midnight or later. It was a schedule that many of her officers and household members found difficult to keep up with. If there had been a prize for hard-working rulers, Mary would easily have beaten out both her fellow monarchs, Emperor Charles V and King Henry II of France.

What followed Mary's announcement was a major uproar. Urged on by Protestant preachers who hated Philip because of his religion, the English reacted as if she had announced she was handing the whole country over to Spain—fields and forests, cows and castles, ships and sheep. It would of course be many months before the actual wedding could take place. First, the two governments had to arrange the marriage treaty, always a complicated business

There was in fact a great deal to be done. The business of running the government had been let slide for many years while the Council members enriched themselves and quarreled with one another. The realm's finances were also in poor shape. Northumberland had left the nation a vast debt of 700,000 pounds, and Mary had to expend a lot of effort in trying to borrow money from the Flemish banking center in Antwerp.

Philip of Spain, at the age of twenty-four, about three years before his marriage to Mary.

(Martin Hume, *Two English Queens and Philip*, 1908)

Of course, the Protestants were right about one thing. Mary *was* bringing the country back to the mass and the Catholic Church, but in her own eyes she was doing it slowly and carefully. However, one issue she had to face right away was the problem of her half-sister Elizabeth. Naturally, the Protestants loved Princess Elizabeth with the same affection the Catholics had previously showered on Mary. Elizabeth's strategy in this situation was not defiance but seeming compliance. She attended mass with Mary, although reluctantly and under pressure. She was very, very discreet about her relations with Protestants. And she avoided, as far as possible, any talk of her own marriage.

As soon after Mary's coronation as seemed decent, Elizabeth left London for her own estates, exchanging a sisterly embrace with Mary and gracefully accepting the queen's gift of two strings of gorgeous pearls and a hood made of sable fur. She probably paid more attention to a parting gift from Councilors Paget and Arundel, who warned her bluntly to stay out of politics. Unlike Mary, Elizabeth had not yet stepped down off the Tudor tightrope.

News of serious trouble over religion first reached the court in mid-January 1554. In Herefordshire (near the Welsh border), in Leicestershire (right in the country's center), and in Kent (just southeast of London), there was armed rebellion. This news was especially alarming because the rebels were so widely scattered. It looked as if the unrest might spread like the plague. Equally disturbing was the fact that some of the rebellion's leaders were well known at court. They included Edward Courtenay, Earl of Devonshire (cheated of an easy kingship by marriage), and the Marquess of Dorset, whom Mary had spared after he tried to set his daughter Jane Grey on the throne only the previous July.

But though most of the leaders were quickly arrested or frightened off, Sir Thomas Wyatt continued to raise the men of Kent in the rebellion's support. Wyatt was the son of a very fine poet of Henry's court—also named Thomas—who had written some lovely lyrics in praise of Queen Ann Boleyn and been lucky to escape with his life when Ann fell from favor. Now the second Thomas was playing on fears of the Spanish, plus religious resentments. In London rumor exaggerated the size of Wyatt's army, suggested that France would invade England, and disagreed as to whether Wyatt was trying to set Jane Grey or Elizabeth on Mary's throne.

Soon, in "weather so terrible that no man could stir by water, nor yet well by land," the tough old Duke of Norfolk (now aged 81) led a force to confront the rebels. But when he arrived, some of his men deserted to join Wyatt. Norfolk's loyal troops were forced to retreat. This was a very bad sign.

Back in London, Mary had no national army other than the 200 archers of her personal guard. Wars at this time were fought by the followers of individual lords and knights, and many of Mary's lords were too far away to reach London in time. Mary called on the City of London to defend itself. Soon every gate was guarded, and guns were set up to protect London Bridge, the only way across the Thames River into the city. As the rebels advanced, Mary's advisers began telling her she ought to leave. She might go to Windsor, hide out in the countryside, or even cross the Channel to the English city of Calais. Other people were leaving by the dozens, after all, and in the back of the Councilors' minds was the thought that the queen was just a woman, who should run for safety. As so often before, they misjudged her.

Mary resolutely refused to leave. Instead, she went to the Guildhall, the seat of the city's government, where a crowd of citizens had gathered. Most wanted to work out a defense plan, but there were some in that high-timbered chamber who were willing to hand the queen over to the rebels.

From the Guildhall's platform, Mary addressed the crowd in her low-pitched, carrying voice. Some historians have called Mary "the Spanish Tudor," but on this day, the queen was entirely English. She had always been good at speaking her mind. Now she told her people the truth as she saw it. "I come unto you in mine own person to tell you that which you already see and know. That is, how traitorously and rebelliously a number of Kentishmen have assembled themselves against both us and you." As Mary went on, the hall was completely quiet.

The Guildhall, London, where Mary spoke to her troops during Wyatt's Rebellion. The building was substantially restored after a fire, and the statues are in a much later style.
(*Pictorial London*, 1906)

"Now, loving subjects," Mary said, "what I am, ye right well know. I am your Queen, to whom at my coronation when I was wedded to the realm and laws of the same...you promised your...obedience....And I say unto you, on the word of a prince [meaning a ruler], I cannot tell how naturally the mother loveth the child, for I was never the mother of any, but certainly if a prince and governor may as naturally and earnestly love her subjects as a mother doth love the child, then assure yourselves that I...do as earnestly and tenderly love and favor you."

If ever she thought that her marriage would harm England, she went on to promise them, she would give up Philip on the spot and remain single the rest of her life. Mary ended with these words: "And now, good subjects, pluck up your hearts, and like true men, stand fast against these rebels...and fear them not, for I assure you, I fear them nothing at all!" As their queen finished speaking, many of the audience members were in tears, and the rest were cheering "God save Queen Mary! God save Queen Mary!"

On Saturday, February 3, 1554, Wyatt's troops arrived on the south side of the Thames, but found that they had fewer guns than the defenders of London Bridge. Mary might have splattered them all over the neighborhood at that point, because the guns of the Tower were aimed right at the area occupied by the rebels. But Mary refused to order her gunners to fire, because "many poor men and householders are like to be undone there and killed." On account of the guns, however, Wyatt decided to lead his men upriver to another crossing and attack at dawn on February 7.

Mary was by now at Westminster, right in the rebels' path, but again she would not run away. Wyatt had entered the actual outskirts of the city, and the situation might have become desperate. Nevertheless, the loyal troops held firm, and other forces closed off all Wyatt's lines of retreat. By five o'clock, he had been forced to surrender.

Other would-be rebel leaders were soon arrested also. Since bearing arms against the queen was clearly treason, Mary could have made her justice a great deal bloodier than it was. Wyatt himself was of course condemned, although Mary was moved by the pleas of his wife and saw to it that the family did not starve. Also arrested was the treacherous Henry Grey, Marquess of Dorset, who had been captured while hiding in a hollow tree. Mary, against advice, had spared Dorset in July, only to have him turn on her again. It was a fatal mistake, not only for Dorset but for his daughter Jane and her husband Guildford. All three died on the block, Jane with great courage and dignity. This was the first Tudor blood Mary had shed. But Mary believed that if Jane were allowed to live, she herself would be in constant fear of a civil war started by Jane's supporters. Mary had learned a bitter lesson. A sizable number of the English people, who had brought her to the throne without loss of a single life, no longer supported her, nor could she trust all her great lords in moments of crisis.

Mary's courts condemned about 114 members of Wyatt's forces. According to the custom of the time, they were publicly executed and their bodies were left to rot as a grim warning to others. Of the remaining leaders, some were caught and tried, while others escaped to France, where they continued to plot against the Spanish marriage or against Mary or both. What caused more comment at the time was the number of people Mary *spared*. On February 22, she pardoned more than 400 ordinary fighting men. Furthermore, the bird-brained Edward Courtenay, who had betrayed his fellow conspirators at the first sign of trouble, was sent into exile after a brief stay in prison. The people and the ballad makers had by this time dubbed her "Mercifull Marye."

But Mary's loss of trust in her people's loyalty was to affect her future actions. Her experience as a leader of rebellious Catholics had made her believe that individuals were either for her or against her. She was not well equipped to deal with shades of gray in personal relationships. Now she was growing distrustful, especially where Princess Elizabeth was concerned. Following the rebellion, Elizabeth was sent to the Tower for three months, and there were many in Mary's Council who recommended death for both her and Courtenay. Ambassador Renard also wanted the pair eliminated. It was perhaps Elizabeth's most frightening moment on the tightrope. Only a frantic letter protesting her loyalty to Mary saved her life—and perhaps the fact that she had done nothing to assist the rebellion, although she probably knew of the plans for it.

Another person who got off easily was Antoine de Noailles, the French ambassador, who had certainly been an enthusiastic supporter of the rebel cause. He didn't know that the queen and Renard had cracked the code in which he reported back to the French king. France was still a Catholic kingdom, but as always in the old triangular game, France would do anything to prevent the forthcoming alliance between England and the Empire.

In March, even before all the captured rebels had been executed, Mary was formally betrothed to Philip. She would have been severely disappointed if she had known that as soon as he had signed the marriage treaty, Philip signed another paper saying he was not bound by its terms. What Philip didn't like about the treaty was that Mary had insisted he have no official power in England (or she in Spain). The treaty also said he couldn't appoint Spaniards to court offices and would have no rights to the English throne if Mary died childless. These provisions were in keeping with Mary's oath to her people. On the other hand, any son of Philip and Mary would inherit both England and the Netherlands, while Philip's son by his first wife would inherit Spain. The fact that Philip was annoyed by these terms shows clearly what a difficult position a woman ruler was in at this time. By law, a husband ruled his wife. By law, a queen ruled her subjects. How could a husband be a subject? The Tudor age had no answer for this contradiction.

Chapter 9

A Saint Who Dresses Badly

*I*n the spring of 1554, all the queen's energy was focused on her upcoming wedding. Mary had quite simply fallen in love with what she heard about Philip. She had waited so long, so very long. And God had sent her a fine Catholic prince who would help her in her task of saving the English from heresy. How could she not love him? How could he not love her? It was unthinkable.

Nevertheless, the weeks and months dragged on and Philip did not come to England. In part it was because he was receiving a constant stream of instructions from his father—how to act, how to dress, what to say, what not to say, what servants to bring, whom not to offend.

Not till July 20 did the Spanish fleet of 125 ships drop anchor at the English port of Southampton, after an eight-day voyage from Spain. Philip's flagship was so gorgeously painted and draped in cloth that it was compared to "a lovely flower garden." The prince had brought 9,000 nobles and servants. There were also 1,000 horses and mules, so with the neighing and braying, the shouting of orders, and the cheering, the scene at the dockside was both noisy and confusing. It was also wet. The Spaniards were getting their first taste of English weather. Philip had to borrow an English cape and hat to protect him from the relentless rain.

The queen herself was waiting two miles away at the palace of Bishop Gardiner in Winchester. Meanwhile in Southampton, Philip received a wedding gift from his father, who sent word that he had made his son King of Naples. This news was very welcome to Philip, since his rank now equaled Mary's.

Mary and Philip did not actually meet until three days later, in the Bishop's palace. British observers noted that he was well built, and although not especially tall, was still taller than the small-boned Mary. The prince, or rather, the King of Naples, was gray-eyed, with blond hair and beard. His manner was royal but also friendly. In other words, he was doing everything he possibly could to "appear to be pleased," as one of his father's officials had advised him. The English, and Mary as well, were very favorably impressed.

Unfortunately, the Spanish were not so pleased with the English queen. Mary's years of worry and hard work, not to mention the stress of the recent rebellion, had marked her 38-year-old face at a time when youth was really over in one's twenties. A Spanish courtier snickered, in one of the cattiest remarks of the decade, "She is a perfect saint, who dresses badly." But then, the Spanish thought all English women dressed badly, which is to say they didn't dress in the Spanish style.

On July 25, Mary and Philip were married in Winchester Cathedral with great pomp. Philip wore white, gold, and crimson. Mary wore black velvet as a foil for her display of jewels and cloth-of-gold mantle, which dazzled everyone present. Nevertheless, her choice of wedding ring was a plain gold band. She explained that she wanted to be married "as maidens were married in the old time."

There followed a wedding feast at which each of the four courses contained thirty dishes and was saluted with bowing and fanfares of trumpets. The guests must have been tired by the banquet's end, for the affair lasted several hours and only the royal couple had chairs. Everyone else at the four long tables ate standing.

According to tradition, this oak chair is the one that Mary used during her wedding ceremony.

(By courtesy of the Dean and Chapter of Winchester Cathedral; photograph by John Crook)

Afterward, there was dancing in one of the bishop's private rooms, where Philip's gentlemen and the queen's ladies tried to make conversation, with little success. Like their master Philip, the Spaniards did not speak any English, and the only way the two groups could successfully exchange chitchat was in Latin.

Mary and Philip ate their suppers (the last meal of the day) in their private rooms, then were conducted to the chamber containing the great, curtained marriage bed, set above the floor on a low platform to avoid drafts. If Mary was nervous about her wedding night with a much younger man, she didn't show it. The bishop blessed the bed and then left the bride and groom alone. Mary had her husband, for whose sake she had stood up against most of her Council, her Parliament, and a good portion of her subjects.

The next morning, the queen's ladies in the privy chamber (meaning the private chamber outside her bedroom door) were shocked to find a group of Philip's gentlemen asking to enter the royal bedchamber. No one had explained to the ladies that it was a Spanish custom to congratulate the bride and groom in bed after the wedding night. The ladies protested this (to them) improper approach, but it turned out the gentlemen were too late anyway. Philip had gotten up at seven and gone to work.

In the days that followed, it was clear to all that Mary was deeply in love with her husband. She said as much in her letters and, although both of them spent many hours in state business, she was never happier than when he was at her side.

Philip continued to act affectionate, tactful, and romantic. His best friend, Ruy Gomez, wrote that "the king is certainly a master hand at it when he cares to try." The point was that for Philip, his marriage was a task, not a treat.

Nevertheless, there were frictions between the two sets of courtiers. The Spanish hated the English weather and food. They thought the English ladies not only dressed unfashionably but were too thin and pale. They said the English were given to gossip, lived in uncomfortable houses, and drank too much.

Similarly, the English disliked the Spaniards' "high and mighty" manners and their smooth, less athletic style of dancing, while envying the fact that they never seemed to run out of money. The result was that quarrels broke out between the Spaniards and their hosts—in taverns, on the streets, and even in the palace itself. Both Mary and Philip issued the strictest orders against such outbreaks, but the insults and brawling continued.

Soon Philip was allowing members of his household to leave England to join the imperial troops in the Netherlands. The truth was, the Spanish were far shorter of money than they appeared to be (having been told to make a fine show for the English). Ruy Gomez quipped, "If the English find out how hard up we are, I doubt whether we shall escape with our lives."

Then, in September, came the good, the wonderful news that Mary was pregnant. Suddenly, all the friction seemed worthwhile. This was what the marriage was supposed to be about, from both the political and the religious point of view. Everyone's mood improved immediately, and courtiers on both sides returned to a wary politeness.

Yet there was still a major bone to pick between England and Spain. Philip had not been crowned king. This problem was to nag at Mary for the rest of her life. Merely by marrying, she had weakened her position. Her Council and many of her people assumed that the real power now resided with Philip, no matter what the marriage treaty said. After all, both the law and the Church agreed that women were less capable than men in every way. It was as if Mary had handed people a license to forget all her achievements—her refusal to crumble under pressure from both Henry and Edward, her prompt action on the death of the young king, her courageous leadership during Wyatt's rebellion. And the situation became worse because Mary was now fighting herself as well. Everything Tudor-age women were taught suggested that their role was to serve and obey their husbands. That had actually been Queen Jane's motto: "Born to Serve and Obey."

Like everyone else of the time, Mary had been raised on traditional stories of women who had given in to their husbands. She also had the example of her own mother, who had declared herself willing to hand over her daughter, her jewels, and her personal freedom to Henry her husband. Katharine's story almost seemed to echo the well-known folktale about Patient Griselda.

This story, as set down in Chaucer's *Canterbury Tales* two centuries before, was exactly the sort of thing that women would have told aloud as they sewed or wove or embroidered. Griselda, the story went, was a lovely maiden of humble birth who was chosen by a great lord to be his wife. But, as a test, her husband took away all her children as soon as they were born. He told her they had been killed, even though in fact they were being raised by a relative. Each time, Griselda bowed to her lord's will, never complaining about his cruel decisions. Finally, as one last trial, her husband announced she wasn't good enough for him, and he sent her back to her father, penniless and almost naked. Yet Griselda went meekly. And of course there was a "happy" ending in which the husband (a self-righteous swine if ever there was one) decided she *was* good enough for him after all and came to take her home to his castle. Believe it or not, Griselda actually went back with him. Even Chaucer had a sense of humor about this story, remarking that he doubted the women of his times (the 1300s) would let themselves be treated this way. But the idea was still very much alive—a good woman should suffer almost any abuse from her husband without complaint.

Queen Mary in her mid-thirties, in a painting from the studio of Antonis Mor. It is not the face of a woman who has had an easy life. (Isabella Stuart Gardner Museum, Boston)

Mary was now caught in an impossible bind. What did she owe to Philip, what did she owe to her Church, and what did she owe to her country, especially when they seemed to pull her in different directions? She would get advice on this and many other matters from one of her oldest and dearest friends. Cardinal Reginald Pole had landed in England on November 20. The trouble was that Pole didn't understand the English situation as well as he thought he did, and his advice to Mary was not always good.

The cardinal's first important duty was to take formal action to end the separation of the English Church from that of Rome. His words were reassuring: "I come to reconcile, not to condemn. I come not to compel, but to call again." Then he spoke about the miracle that had peacefully ended the former division—a miracle brought about by their queen when she was only "a virgin, helpless, naked, and unarmed." This description was intended as a compliment and probably was one in the opinion of Pole's audience. But it completely misrepresented Mary and reduced her to the level of a puppet. In fact, Mary was not helpless because she had a good brain and a gift for argument. She was not naked because she was armored with a stout Tudor will to win. And she was not unarmed as long as she had the courage to face danger and inspire others to do the same. To believe Pole's well-meaning words was to shake her confidence and make her task harder.

The biggest stumbling block to restoring the Catholic Church was the people who had taken possession of the rich abbeys and priories that had been dissolved under King Henry. They might profess to be good Catholics now, but they were not at all willing to give their grain fields, cattle, sheep, geese, water mills, tenant farms, gardens, orchards, and buildings back to any church. Return of Church lands was a much bigger issue than the mass itself. Nevertheless, Parliament quickly acted to adopt Roman Catholicism as the national religion. It also restored some ancient laws that set the punishment for heresy, meaning any religious belief that was not approved by the Church. At the time, the heresy law did not attract much attention. It was just part of putting things back the way they had been.

*Cardinal Reginald Pole,
an adviser who saw only
one side of the religious
question.*
(Martin Hume, *Two English
Queens and Philip*, 1908)

The restoration of the Old Religion was one of Mary's happiest moments. She had done the one thing she believed God had chosen her to do. And to double God's blessing, she was joyfully, miraculously pregnant despite her age, just like Abraham's wife Sarah in the Bible, who bore a child when she was ninety.

Nevertheless, there was still discontent among the country's many Protestants. A few churches were burned, and some people were even attacked for speaking in favor of the mass. Rumors began to spread. The monks and nuns would come back. Philip's troops would seize the former Church lands by force. The Spanish were going to take over the government. Many Protestants left the country, fearing heresy charges. Not that the Protestants believed burning heretics was wrong—they just had a different way of defining heresy.

The protests and violence in England brought about the first public burnings of heretics. Highest in rank was John Hooper, Bishop of Worcester. Hooper held strongly Protestant views and had called many

Catholic teachings ridiculous. Hooper refused to change his mind and save his life. He suffered a slow and horrible death on a February morning in 1555, crying out, "For God's love, good people, let me have more fire" (meaning die more quickly). At the time, very few thought burning heretics was anything but fair punishment. The argument made in favor of these executions was that they would save lives by making other people respect the religious laws. Philip did urge caution in condemning people for heresy, but only because he didn't want to upset the English. In Europe, his father the Emperor Charles had already killed at least 30,000 Anabaptists and Lutherans, while the Spanish Inquisition (a religious court) continued to seek out not only Protestants but Jews for torture and execution.

Mary's own attitude to heresy was that most Protestants had been led astray by a few bad preachers and bishops. Those men and women who "by learning should seek to deceive the simple" ought to be condemned, but "without rashness." The queen did not know how wrong she was about Protestantism. Its followers were not few, they were many. They were not being misled by bad preachers; they truly believed. And they were not simple, but came from all ranks of society and levels of education.

By Easter time, Mary and Philip had moved to Hampton Court. The palace's famous gardens offered pleasant walkways, both open and covered, and beds of flowers planted in complex patterns like knots. All around this garden were what in Henry's day had been called "the king's beasts." Made of wood, the brightly painted lions, falcons, unicorns, dragons, stags, and many other creatures held in their paws, hoofs, or claws the royal coats of arms. There were stone beasts on the palace itself, too. All in all, it was a bright and cheerful place for Mary's "lying in," the forty days when a royal lady took to her rooms to await the birth of a child. Mary's child was expected in May of 1555. Philip was planning to stay in England until after the birth, which relieved Mary of one major worry—that her husband would be absent on the day when she presented the realm with an heir.

Hampton Court Palace, along the Thames River. Cardinal Wolsey built this magnificent residence while he was Lord Chancellor. When he began to lose favor with Henry VIII, Wolsey was "encouraged" to give the palace to the King. Hampton Court was familiar to Mary throughout her life. Portions of the building are later additions, and of course the little steam launch in the foreground is from the early 1900s.
(*Pictorial London,* 1906)

For months, Mary's women had been sewing clothes for the baby and smocks for the queen, all embroidered with silk and silver thread. The birthing room and the royal nursery were swept and decorated with fresh hangings and cloths of estate. There was also a cradle with a painted verse asking health and long life for "the Child whom Thou to Mary, O God of Might, has send."

Sadly, however, all these preparations were in vain. Even though, according to her doctors, Mary had shown all the signs of pregnancy, she was not pregnant and never had been. The swelling of her figure may have been due to a tumor or a cyst or some other cause, but there was no child. A few courtiers (such as de Noailles, the French ambassador) had begun to suspect this as early as the previous winter. No one would have dared to suggest such a thing to Mary, however. Both her doctors and her women went along with the idea that a baby would soon be coming, although some, who loved her best, were afraid for her life. In those days, not many women survived the birth of a first child at 39.

The summer of 1555 was altogether awful for Mary and for England. The weather was so wet that the crops could not ripen, and farm animals died of disease. Everyone foresaw hard times in the coming winter. At court, Philip was bored, short of money, and anxious to leave for Flanders as soon as possible.

By August, even Mary was forced to give up the idea that she was pregnant and return to the daily business of the court. Her prayer book from this period still survives. Its pages show signs of much use and are spotted as if by tears. She had lost both her child and her husband, as Philip was eager to set out for Flanders. Mary decided to ride with him as far as Greenwich. She drew joyful crowds along their route. One of the many recent rumors had been that the queen was dead.

On August 26, Philip sailed, and as soon as he arrived in the Netherlands, he became extremely busy. Emperor Charles had decided to retire and hand over the Netherlands to Philip, but this was easier said than done. Philip had months of paperwork, proclamations, and ceremonies to get through. It did not help Mary's state of mind to learn that her beloved husband was going out masked almost every evening, attending banquets, drinking a good deal of strong Flemish beer, and generally enjoying himself. Nevertheless, she wrote to him daily, begging for his quick return, and sent him a batch of the meat pies he especially liked.

Sometimes people recreate their parents' lives without meaning to. Just then, Mary's feelings for Philip echoed what Katharine had written to Henry on her deathbed: "Mine eyes desire you above all things."

During Philip's absence abroad, he had told Mary's trusted adviser Cardinal Pole, that he, Pole, was more or less in charge of the country. Nevertheless, both Pole and Philip were amazed at Mary's hard work and zeal for meeting with her Council, hearing petitions from her subjects, and drafting official documents. Mary was always well informed because she liked to read all the letters to and from her ambassadors abroad.

Yet it must be said that Mary did not have the knack of getting her Councilors—with their differing opinions and interests—to work together. Her experience of leadership had always meant leading those who already agreed with her and taking stands that were moral, not political. Her tactic of just saying no to her opponents worked well when she was heroically defending Catholics' right to worship as their consciences dictated. This same tactic was not as effective when she needed alternately to praise, threaten, or compromise in order to accomplish the work of governing. Mary never really controlled her Council, which constantly bickered and occasionally ignored her wishes.

As the year wore on, Mary became distressed at Philip's continuing absence. Philip didn't even write as often as she would have liked, and when he did, it was to complain that he had no reason to come back to England since she had not seen fit to arrange his coronation.

As time went on and England got used to the idea that Mary was not likely to produce an heir, the queen's relationship with her half-sister Elizabeth became more and more difficult. Elizabeth was widely believed to be a Protestant, although she attended Catholic services when she was at Mary's court. Her youth was her greatest weapon against Mary because she might well be more successful in producing an heir. Whenever discontented Protestants gathered to talk politics in cellars or chapels or the back rooms of taverns, the first name they mentioned was Elizabeth's. The second, as often as not, was that of Edward Courtenay, Earl of Devonshire. Courtenay, who was at that time living in Venice, Italy, had recently (and very conveniently) decided to become a Protestant.

Many people (including Courtenay) thought this made him a perfect match for Elizabeth. Philip's friend Ruy Gomez was so alarmed at the threat to Philip and Mary that he hatched a murder-for-hire scheme against Courtenay. The plot involved a Dalmatian soldier and some Venetian outlaws; the price was a thousand crowns. However, the soldier wisely told the Venetians all about it, and Courtenay continued to live, causing trouble for Mary by his very existence.

The mood of the country worsened as more Protestants were burned as heretics. One enthusiastic supporter of the burnings was Edmund Bonner, Bishop of London. Bonner had been imprisoned in the Tower during Edward's reign, but the experience had not made him more merciful. Fat, greedy, and fond of dirty jokes, Bonner became a much-hated figure. Children on the streets of London shouted, "Bloody Bonner!" as he passed by.

The execution of Archbishop Cranmer, March 21, 1556, as illustrated in Foxe's book on the "English martyrs."

Among those who were condemned by Bonner was Thomas Cranmer, former Archbishop of Canterbury. Cranmer's death was particularly moving because while in prison this very human man gave in and accepted Catholicism. Mary, however, did not believe his change of heart was sincere. The fact that she had been just as insincere when she gave in to Henry in 1536 did not lead her to pardon him. She believed, quite simply, that her religious beliefs were right and Cranmer's were wrong. She allowed the execution to go ahead. When Cranmer found out there was to be no pardon for him, he withdrew his earlier confessions, declaring that they went against his conscience. At the stake, he held out his right hand to the fire, saying it deserved to burn first because it had signed the papers. More than twenty years before, Cranmer had helped King Henry with his divorce from Katharine of Aragon. Now the cause of English Protestantism had become one that many were ready to die for.

In all, about 300 English Protestants died at the stake rather than give up their religious beliefs. Only a handful were ladies and gentlemen of social rank. Nearly all were ordinary working people—farmers, weavers, wagon makers, and such. Sadly, these were the same sort of people whom Mary had freely pardoned after Wyatt's Rebellion. She found it easier to forgive rebels against her own rule than rebels against the Church.

Even among English Catholics, the burnings had little popular support. In areas such as London and Kent, where Protestantism was strong, crowds came to shout prayers and encouragement to the victims. "God strengthen them," one voice would call, and the crowd would cry out, "Amen."

The "fires of Smithfield" (the place where many of the burnings took place) became a byword and a symbol of these persecutions. Much of Mary's popularity among the common people of southeastern England went up in the smoke from these terrible fires.

Many Protestants fled England, seeking refuge in Switzerland and other Protestant states. As a group, they became known as the "Marian exiles." One of the most prominent was John Foxe. His *Acts and Monuments of the English Martyrs* described the deaths of John Hooper, Thomas

Cranmer, and others in sensational detail. "Foxe's Book of Martyrs," as it is frequently called, remained in print for centuries and convinced whole generations of readers that Mary Tudor was a bloody tyrant.

Looking back, it is easy to see that Mary's greatest flaw was that she could not understand the similarity between her own earlier position under the Protestant Council and that of the Protestants under Catholic authority. Mary had heard of the executions of men like Sir Thomas More (later a Catholic saint) and wondered if she would be next. But her character and life experiences had made her into a person who did not bend or compromise in the face of opposition. It was both her strength and her weakness.

Chapter 10

War, and Peace

Mary was now struggling with two major issues: her husband and her sister. She still missed Philip and dreamed of his return. People were comparing her to Queen Dido of Carthage, who pined for the hero Aeneas in an ancient Latin poem, *The Aeneid*. Aeneas had sailed off to Italy to found Rome. Philip was not founding Rome. Instead, before the end of the year, one of his commanders would attack it.

Oddly enough, it was a threat of war with Rome that brought Mary and Philip back together. Since 1555, the pope had been Paul IV. Paul came from Naples, which had earlier been seized by Spain, and he loathed everything and everyone Spanish. Paul was a fierce and angry old man who still had the vigor of someone half his age. He quickly made an alliance with Philip's rivals the French and arrested several of the Empire's officials, locking them up in the Castel Sant' Angelo, Rome's version of the Tower of London. Furious, Philip sent his commander the Duke of Alva to attack the country around Rome. Pope Paul then excommunicated Philip.

It was a serious crisis, but Mary had lived with crisis all her life. Catholics believed that popes as individuals could make mistakes, and Mary thought this was a big one. Loyally, she rallied her resources to help Philip, sending him reports from her agents abroad and a considerable sum of money. Then, on March 18, 1557, after an absence of a year and a half, Philip came back to England. At this point, Philip needed Mary more than he ever had before.

In preparing for war, Philip and Mary were helped by at least one thing. The weather of 1557 was excellent, and it looked as if the harvest would be a fat one. While she could, Mary enjoyed Philip's company, working hard (as they were both accustomed to do), but also riding out with him to hunt in the green and flowering countryside. That summer she rode with him to the harbor at Dover, too, when Philip left to fight the French. But Mary had something to console her for his absence because, by December 1557, she was again firmly convinced she was pregnant.

On the other side of the Channel, Philip won a significant battle against the French at St. Quentin. About the same time, his commander the Duke of Alva made peace terms with Pope Paul. To Philip, it seemed the war was over. But the French had not made peace with England and, through the clever use of spies and leaking false information, they managed to capture Calais, a fortified town on the coast of France that the English had held for centuries.

News of the fall of Calais, on January 7, 1558, hit the English very hard. Once, England had ruled a broad swath of land in western France. Calais was an important symbol of English power because it was the last little bit of those rich territories. The English felt that this loss was Mary's fault because the war had been for her husband's benefit. They were largely right. Philip, however, declared that though he regretted Calais, he was much cheered by Mary's pregnancy, which had become public knowledge.

At this point, counting forward from last July, when Philip had left England, Mary's child should have been due to be born. But this time, too, Mary was to be disappointed. However, she took no time off to rest, calm down, and recover. Instead, she threw herself right back into the stressful work of attempting to control her quarrelsome and divided Council, where everyone was trying to blame everyone else for the loss of Calais.

It now seemed clear that Mary would not produce an heir and that she was seriously ill as well. The court naturally looked around to see who would rule next. The act of Parliament that restored the terms of Henry VIII's will had also restored Elizabeth as heir to the throne. Mary herself resisted this idea for years, but naming anyone else would have brought civil war. For example, the young and Catholic Mary Stuart, Queen of Scots, would have brought England under the domination of her husband, Francis, who was heir to the throne of hated France.

Just as Mary herself had been during Edward's reign, Princess Elizabeth was now loved by the English people. In the latter part of 1556, she had arrived for a stay at court with the same cheering crowds and public praise that had greeted Mary in the spring of 1551. Even Philip was paying attention to Elizabeth—so much so that there were rumors of an affair. But Elizabeth was not about to get tangled up with lovers or suitors. She was biding her time, as Mary had done. When Elizabeth heard that Mary was ill during the spring and summer of 1558, the 25-year-old princess kept her own counsel.

By August, Mary was worse. It's impossible now to say what Mary's actual illness was. She may have had ovarian cancer or one of several other problems. By October, however, it was clear to her doctors that Mary's condition was very grave. Mary herself agreed, and she wrote an addition to her will that provided for her most loyal friends. It seemed death was all around her. Both the Emperor Charles and his sister died in October, and Reginald Pole would outlive Mary only by hours.

In the month of November, Mary's greatest comfort was to hear mass. She was called now to lay down the burden of ruling. The little girl who never cried had shed many tears as an adult, but she had done her best, her very best as she understood it. She died peacefully on the morning of November 17, 1558, just after hearing mass and repeating the Latin responses, "Have mercy on us, Have mercy on us, Give us peace."

None of us hears what is said about us after we die, and that is sometimes just as well. Certainly it was a kindness that Mary never knew Philip's response to news of her death. She had willed him several important jewels, including the enormous diamond that had been his betrothal gift to her, but all he could think of to say about her death was, "I felt a reasonable regret."

Far more charitable, and courageous under the circumstances, were the words spoken at Mary's funeral by the Bishop of Winchester. After the procession arrived at Westminster Cathedral, with Mary's household gentlemen in black, with her gold-embroidered banners and the carved funeral image crowned and dressed in crimson, the bishop had this to say: "She was never unmindful or uncareful of her promise to her realm. She used singular mercy toward offenders. She used much pity and compassion towards the poor and oppressed....I verily believe the poorest creature in this city feared not God more than she did."

Then her officers broke their staffs of office and, according to long-established tradition, threw them into the grave. This time, however, the action was more than a gesture. They all knew that the next ruler was most unlikely to reappoint them.

Elizabeth Tudor was now Queen of England, and her reign would be long, brilliant, and glorious. Like Mary, however, she would be threatened by rebellions and plots on the part of those opposed to her religion—Protestantism this time. Like Mary, she would execute one of her cousins (Mary Stuart, Queen of Scots) for conspiring to take her throne. And like Mary, she would burn her share of people because of their religion, about 200 in all.

As long as the state supported one form of religion over another, heresy trials and religious wars would disrupt the peace of Europe and cause untold suffering. It was precisely these historic scenes that the authors of the United States Constitution had in mind when they forbade Congress to interfere with religious freedom or establish an official religion.

In the end, Mary must answer to history for the Protestants she allowed to be sent to their deaths. But did Mary deserve the title "bloody"? That seems hard to justify. The 1500s were after all a bloody age, in which there were dozens of crimes for which one could be executed, some of them as small as stealing a shilling's worth of food. Mary believed God had called her to bring back the Catholic faith in England, and she had done that, although the tide was running toward Protestantism. She had restored honor to her beloved mother Katharine. She had been brave, stubborn, loving, angry, merciful, and unforgiving. It was Protestant historians who wrote the story of Mary's reign and gave her the title Bloody Mary. But the word most often used to describe her during her lifetime, by those who knew her best, was "gentle."

Great Britain under the Tudors

KEY
★ Capital city
† Archbishopric
• City
▪ Manor house or royal residence

SCOTLAND
Edinburgh

Carlisle   Durham

Irish Sea

YORKSHIRE
†York

North Sea

Humber R.

Lincoln

WALES

ENGLAND

Norwich   Yarmouth

Ludlow   Kenninghall

Severn R.

Kimbolton   Framlingham

St. Davids

Wye R.

Hatfield House   Hunsdon

Thames R.   London

Bristol   Windsor   Greenwich   †Canterbury

Hampton   Richmond   KENT
Court

CORNWALL   Winchester

Exeter

NETHERLANDS

FLANDERS

Calais   Brussels

English Channel

FRANCE

ATLANTIC
OCEAN

N

0   50   100 mi.
0   80   160 km

Paris ★

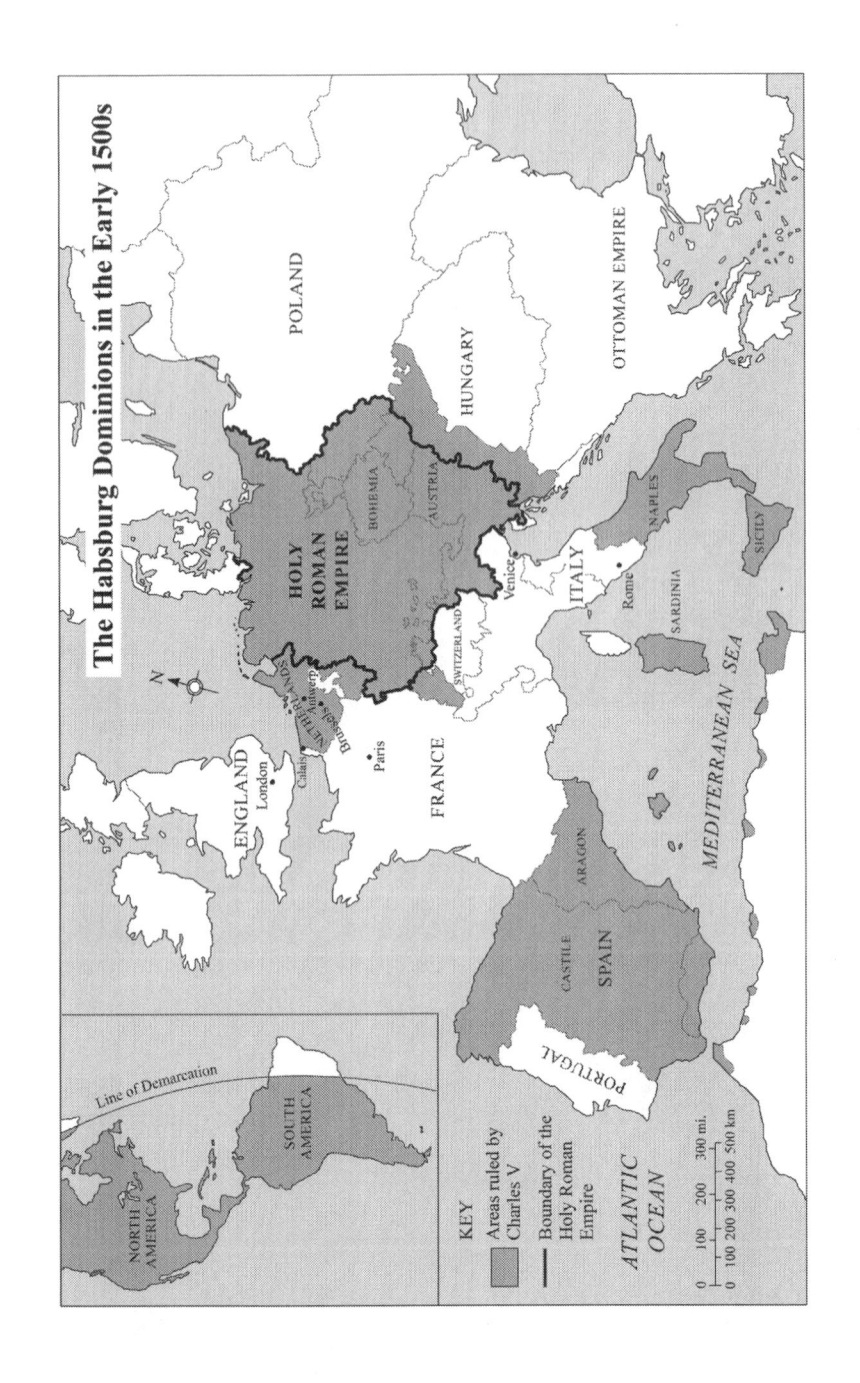

The Habsburg Dominions in the Early 1500s

Mary Tudor's Family Connections

Mary's British Relatives

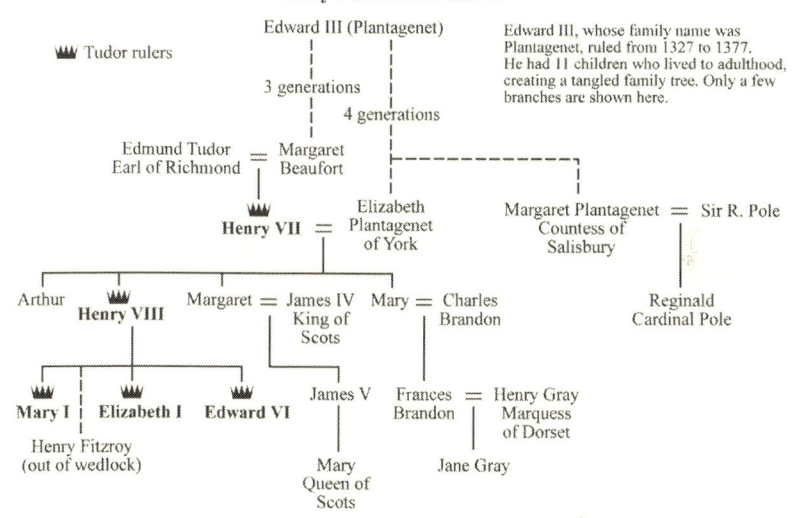

Edward III, whose family name was Plantagenet, ruled from 1327 to 1377. He had 11 children who lived to adulthood, creating a tangled family tree. Only a few branches are shown here.

Mary's Spanish Relatives

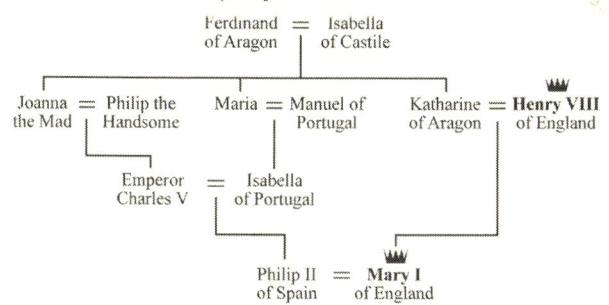

Author's Note on Names

People's names of the 1500s are confusing for two reasons. First of all, spelling was extremely variable. The same person might sign her name (if she could write at all) as Margarete Smith one day and Margret Smythe the next. This makes matters especially difficult when it comes to the names of the six wives of Henry VIII, who had only three first names among them. To simplify things, I have settled on the following spellings: Katharine of Aragon, Ann Boleyn, Jane Seymour (she's no problem), Anna of Cleves, Kathryn Howard, and Catherine Parr. However, it is important to remember that all these women could and did use different spellings at different times.

The second problem is with titles. Great nobles were often given new lands and titles as marks of royal favor during their careers. An example is John Dudley, the second Lord Protector during the reign of young Edward VI. Dudley was first Viscount Lisle, then Earl of Warwick, then Duke of Northumberland. In all such cases, I have settled on one title (not always the last or highest one borne by the individual) and used it throughout, to avoid confusion. Readers should be aware, however, that reference books and general histories often refer to the same person by more than one title, depending on the date being written about.

Index

Available soon, the next title in this series—

Foremost of Women
A LIFE OF HATSHEPSUT, PHARAOH OF EGYPT

For information on other women rulers from many times and places, see our website at www.WomenWhoLead.org.

0-595-31254-3

6985555R00087

Printed in Great Britain
by Amazon.co.uk, Ltd.,
Marston Gate.